NO. 1

The first book featuring Ben, the lovable, humorous ex-sailor and down-at-heels rascal who can't help running into trouble.

Son of novelist Benjamin Farjeon, and brother to children's author Eleanor, playwright Herbert and composer Harry, Joseph Jefferson Farjeon (1883–1955) began work as an actor and freelance journalist before inevitably turning his own hand to writing fiction. Described by the *Sunday Times* as 'a master of the art of blending horrors with humour', Farjeon was a prolific author of mystery novels, with more than 60 books published between 1924 and 1955. His first play, *No. 17*, was produced at the New Theatre in 1925, when the actor Leon M. Lion 'made all London laugh' as Ben the tramp, an unorthodox amateur detective who became the most enduring of all Farjeon's creations. Rewritten as a novel in 1926 and filmed by Alfred Hitchcock six years later, with Mr Lion reprising his role, *No.17*'s success led to seven further books featuring the warm-hearted but danger-prone Ben: 'Ben is not merely a character but a parable—a mixture of Trimalchio and the Old Kent Road, a notable coward, a notable hero, above all a supreme humourist' (Seton Dearden, *Time and Tide*). Although he had become largely forgotten over the 60 years since his death, J. Jefferson Farjeon's reputation made an impressive resurgence in 2014 when his 1937 Crime Club book *Mystery in White* was reprinted by the British Library, returning him to the bestseller lists and resulting in readers wanting to know more about this enigmatic author from the Golden Age of detective fiction.

Also in this series

No. 17
The House Opposite
Murderer's Trail
Ben Sees It Through
Little God Ben
Detective Ben
Ben on the Job
Number Nineteen

J. JEFFERSON FARJEON

No. 17

COLLINS
CRIME
CLUB

COLLINS CRIME CLUB
An imprint of HarperCollins*Publishers*
1 London Bridge Street
London SE1 9GF
www.harpercollins.co.uk

This paperback edition 2016

First published in Great Britain by Hodder & Stoughton 1926

A catalogue record for this book is
available from the British Library

ISBN 978-0-00-815588-9

Set in Sabon by Palimpsest Book Production Limited, Falkirk, Stirlingshire

Printed in Great Britain by Clays Ltd, St Ives plc

FSC™ is a non-profit international organisation established to promote the responsible management of the world's forests. Products carrying the FSC label are independently certified to assure consumers that they come from forests that are managed to meet the social, economic and ecological needs of present and future generations, and other controlled sources.

Find out more about HarperCollins and the environment at
www.harpercollins.co.uk/green

Contents

Foreword

I usually avoid dedications because, if they are not bare statements, they are too apt to involve a grace of florid expression at variance with sincerity; but this novel seems to me to be insisting on a few words, since it is based on a play the success of which has formed one of the happiest and most important milestones of my career. At once, however, I find myself confounded. To whom shall I dedicate the book? To my wife, who shares with me the fruits of this success? To Mr Leon M. Lion, whose skill and experience materialised those fruits? To the actors and actresses, without whose co-operation all this good fortune could not have been achieved? Or to the original 'Ben,' who could never have been born in my mind had I not met him somewhere—but I cannot say where—on some uncharted, unrecorded journey?

The task of selection is beyond me. In joyous despair I dedicate this book to all!

J.J.F.

1

Figures in the Fog

Fog had London by the throat. It blinded its eyes and muffled its ears. Such traffic as was not at a standstill groped its way with scarcely a sound through the jaundiced streets, and to cross a road was no longer a casual matter, but an adventure into the unknown. For this reason, the timid stayed indoors, while the more daring, and those who had no choice, groped gingerly along the pavements. The pickpockets were busy.

But it is not in the heart of London that our story commences. The fog had stretched its fingers far and wide, and a man who was approaching along one of the arteries that led Londonwards from the north-east paused for a few moments to rub his eyes, and then his stubby chin.

'Gawd 'elp us!' he muttered, staring into the great, gloomy smudge ahead of him. 'If that ain't the Yeller Peril, wot is?'

He had trudged out of a land of sunshine into a land of white mist, and now the white mist was becoming opaque orange. The prospect was so thoroughly unappetising that he even considered the idea of turning back. Had he known what awaited him in that gloomy smudge he would have acted very promptly on the idea, but the future itself is as impenetrable as a fog, and he decided to go on.

'Arter all,' he argued to himself, 'one plice is as good as another, when you ain't got nowhere helse!'

So he lit his best cigarette—barely more than half of it had been smoked by its previous owner—and resumed his way.

A figure suddenly loomed towards him, out of the mist.

'Oi!' exclaimed our traveller, and jumped. His nerves were never of the best, and hunger was beginning to tell on him. But he reacted quickly, and grinned as the figure stopped. 'Why didn't yer sound yer 'ooter?'

The figure grinned, too.

'A bit thick, mate, isn't it?' said the stranger.

'Thick as cheese. Cheese! Lummy, I wish I '*ad* a bit o' cheese!'

'Hungry?'

'Not 'arf! Yer ain't got sich a thing as a leg o' beef on yer, I s'pose?'

The other laughed.

'There's an inn a little way up the road.'

'Ah! Well, jest run back and tell 'em to put dahn the red carpet, will yer? Ben, o' the Merchant Service, is a-comin'. And 'e's got fourpence to spend. Oi! Where yer goin'? Oi!'

The stranger had turned, and darted off. Ben, of the Merchant Service, stared after him.

'Well, if that don't tike the bloomin' ticket!' he murmured. 'Seemed like as if 'e thort I meant it!'

Once more, an instinct rose in him to turn back. He was just entering the fringe of the thick fog belt, and its uncanniness depressed him. He recalled that the stranger had stood almost next to him, yet he had not seen his face. Out of the fog he had come, and back into the fog he had returned. A shadow with a voice—that was all.

But the glory of the Merchant Service, however humble your position in it, must be maintained. You could not let it down; not, at least, until you were *sure* you were going to get hurt! And, after all, what was a little bit of fog? So, deriding himself for his fears, the subtle source of which he was not fitted to understand, he again ignored the kindly warning, and resumed his onward trudge.

The thought of the inn a little way up the road certainly did something to dissipate the gloom. Fourpence wouldn't go far, but a friendly innkeeper might make it go a little further. Then he might earn a few coppers by doing something. You never knew. Ben, of the Merchant Service—perhaps it should be explained, *late* of the Merchant Service—was not in love with work. The stomach, however, drives.

He came upon the inn abruptly. All meetings are abrupt in a fog. It loomed up, a vague, shadowy outline, on his right, and a feeble lamp burned over the door. Ben plunged his hand into his pocket, to corroborate his impression of his bank balance, found the impression correct, and entered.

If he hoped to escape the fog inside, he was disappointed. The bar parlour was full of it. A cough directed him to the counter, and he found a young woman peering at him with half-frowning eyes.

'It's orl right, miss,' Ben assured her. 'I ain't no matinay idol, but then, on the hother 'and, I ain't so bad as I looks. 'Ow far'll fourpence go?'

The young woman smiled, glanced towards an inner room, and then turned back to Ben.

'Fourpence don't go far,' she commented.

'It ain't so dusty, miss, with a bit o' good nacher thrown hin,' said Ben slyly.

'How do you know I've got any good nature?' she retorted.

'It's a guess, miss. But I reckon it's a good 'un. Any'ow, I'll see yer doesn't lose by it. I'll leave yer me di'mond studs in me will.'

Her smile grew more friendly, but once more she glanced towards the inner room. Ben began to grow vaguely uneasy.

'Wotcher got in there, miss?' he asked. 'A hogre?'

The woman shook her head, as though impatient with herself.

'No—just another customer,' she replied.

'Then wotcher keep on—'

'Nothing! What do yer want for your fourpence?'

'Soup, fish, cut orf the joint, and a couple o' veg.,' grinned Ben cheekily.

'Go on—you don't want much, do you?' laughed the woman. 'Well, I must say, you look as if you could do with it. I'll see what I can manage. Get in there.'

'Eh? Wot's that?' jerked Ben.

He glanced towards the door of the inner room, at which she was pointing.

'What's the matter?' she demanded. 'He won't eat you!'

''Oo sed 'e would?' retorted Ben, and shuffled towards the door.

The door was closed, and he opened it slowly and cautiously. Whatever the young woman might say, something was disturbing her, and that something was in the inner room. All right, then. No one was afraid. Just the same, it didn't harm to be careful, did it?

When he had opened the door a little more than a crack, he paused. Two seconds of inaction went by. Then he whispered over his shoulder, to the young woman.

'Ain't yer givin' us a light?'

'Don't be silly,' replied the woman. 'Isn't a lamp good enough?'

'There ain't no lamp, miss!'

'No lamp? Here, you *do* want something to eat. Open the door a bit wider, then you'll see.'

'I tells yer, there ain't *no* light!' whispered Ben. 'And I ain't goin'—'

He stopped abruptly. The woman stared at him, now frankly uneasy. Her mouth remained half open, while five more inactive seconds went by. Then, suddenly, a violent shiver revivified the statuesque figure of Ben, and he swiftly and silently closed the door.

'Goodness, what's that?' asked the woman, with her hand at her heart.

Ben slithered to a seat, and, sitting down abruptly, blinked at her.

'What is it, what is it?' repeated the woman, in a low voice.

'I ain't goin' in there,' muttered Ben.

'For goodness' sake—'

'I'll tell yer, miss. Jest a minit. Sorter took me in the wind, like . . . There *wasn't* no light, see? Wot I ses. If you've give 'im one, 'e's put it aht. And orl I sees, miss, when I looks in that there room, was nothin' . . . nothin' . . .'

'All right, I heard you the first time,' interposed the woman. 'Don't give me the creeps! Oh, dear, I wish father was home, that I do. Well—what made you shut the door so quick?'

Ben looked at her, slightly injured.

'Ain't I tellin' yer?' he demanded. 'Orl right, then. I sees nothin', as I ses. But then, sudden like, I sees—somethin'. It's a figger. Your customer, I reckons, miss. But 'e ain't sittin' at the table. 'E ain't doin' that.'

'What's he doing, then?'

''E seems to be listenin', miss,' said Ben sepulchrally. 'Standin' by the wall, 'e is, listenin', miss . . . listenin' . . .'

'Oh, hark to the man!' gasped the young woman, with her eyes on the door. 'Now he's off again!'

'Yus, but that ain't orl,' he went on. 'I sees the winder. Lummy, I sees the winder. And orl of a suddin, another figger outside pops up agin' it, and shoves 'is fice agin' the glass.' The woman stifled a little shriek, while Ben took out a large red handkerchief and mopped his brow. 'So, arter that,' he concluded, 'I closes the door, and comes away. And so'd anyone.'

There was a short pause. The young woman appeared undecided what to do.

'What did he look like—the man at the window?' she asked.

'Nothin'. Yer couldn't see,' replied Ben. 'Jest shadders, both on 'em. Wot do they call them black things? Sillyhetts, don't they? Well, that's what they was. A couple o' sillyhetts. But—I dunno,' he added reflectively. 'I did seem ter reckernise that chap at the winder—in a kind 'f a way. Seemed like a feller I met up the road. Some'ow. I dunno.' A practical streak entered into him. 'Wotcher goin' ter do, miss? Go in and light 'is lamp for 'im agin?'

'Not me!' she retorted.

''Corse not,' agreed Ben. 'And no more ain't I goin' in there to heat my Carlton lunch!'

'You can eat it in here, if you like.'

'Yus, I do like. Though, mind yer, miss—if it wasn't fer you, I'd 'ook it.'

The young woman looked at Ben a little more intently after this frank statement, and a new light came into her eye.

'You haven't got no call to stay here for me,' she said, watching him.

'Yus, I 'ave,' he responded. 'The call o' the Merchant Service.'

'Oh! Are you in the Merchant Service, then?'

'Well, speakin' strict, miss,' answered Ben carefully, 'I 'ave bin. And 'opes ter be agin. But, jest nah . . . get me?'

'I see,' she nodded. 'You're out of a job.'

'That's right. Man o' lesher.'

'Well, I've got a brother in the Merchant Service, and you can keep your fourpence,' said the young woman. 'I ain't going to charge you for your Carlton lunch, as you call it. You stay here till my father returns, that's all I ask.'

'And yer doesn't hask in vain,' exclaimed Ben roundly. 'I'll proteck yer. Oh, my Gawd, wot's that?'

The door of the inner room flew open, a figure darted across the floor, and vanished through the porch.

2

Enter No. 17

Ben stared at the street door, now open wide, and then at the young woman, whose hands were clasped in fright. Ben's own heart was beating somewhat rapidly.

'Was that yer customer, miss?' he asked.

'Yes,' she gasped. 'Oh, dear! What's it all mean?'

Ben had a theory, but, before expounding it, he played for security. Both the street door and the door to the inner room were open. They required closing.

He walked to the street door first. He peered cautiously out into the wall of yellow, coughed, drew his head in again, and closed the door. Then, even more cautiously, he shuffled across to the inner room, a small portion of which was dimly discernible through the aperture.

'Is anybody in there?' whispered the woman.

'If there is, 'e can blinkin' well stay!' Ben whispered back, as he whipped the door to and locked it. 'The on'y chap it'd be is that chap wot was at the winder, and if 'e come *hin* at the winder, then 'e can go *hout* o' the winder. I reckon that's fair, ain't it?'

'Yes,' murmured the woman. 'Why do you suppose he ran out like that?'

''Cos 'e was runnin' away from somebody,' answered Ben obviously, 'and the somebody was the chap at the winder. Pline as a pikestaff, ain't it? 'Ide and seek in the fog. Yus, and *you* thort somethin' was hup afore I come along, didn't yer?'

'Yes,' she nodded. 'He acted so peculiar.'

''Ow—peckyewlier?'

'Well, he put his head in first, and had a quick look round. Then he went out again, and then he came in again. "Say, give me something to eat," he says, "and I've no time to waste." One of those Yanks. I never did like them. And in he goes to that room just as if the whole place belonged to him.'

'That's a Yank,' said Ben.

'And once, when my back was turned,' she went on, 'he came out of the room quietly, and gave me such a turn. He went to have a look out of the front door, and I said, "Isn't the fog awful?" just to make conversation, and he grinned and replied, "I like it." "I like it," he said, and then went back to the room sudden, as if it was a joke, Of course, I thought I was just silly,' she concluded, 'thinking that way about him. But, you see, I wasn't!'

'No, you wasn't,' agreed Ben. ''E's a wrong 'un.'

He glanced uneasily at the door of the inner room, and the young woman followed his glance.

'I say,' she said quietly. 'Suppose there *is* somebody in there?'

'That's why I locked it,' replied Ben.

'Yes—but oughtn't we to go in and have a look round?'

'Not till I've got somethin' in me stummick. Wot abart that Carlton lunch, miss?'

'Yes—in a minute,' she answered, her eyes still glued on the door. 'I think we ought to have that look round first, though.'

'Wrong order, miss,' Ben assured her. 'Eat fust, 'eroism arterwards. It's a motter in the Merchant Service.'

But she hardly listened to him. In spite of her fear, a sense of duty was reasserting itself within her, and Ben noted this transition with inward misgivings.

'You wait a minute,' murmured the young woman, coming away from the counter. 'I'm going to open that door!'

Ben protested.

'Wait a minit yerself,' he said. 'Ye'r' actin' silly.'

'No, I'm not! Unless you mean I'm acting silly standing here, doing nothing.'

''Ere! 'Arf a mo'!' gasped Ben, as she made another movement towards the locked door. 'I'll *show* yer ye'r' silly, if yer like.'

'Go on, then,' she answered, pausing. 'But be quick about it.'

'It don't tike two ticks. Fust, s'pose there ain't nothin' in that there room?'

'I don't suppose there will be.'

'Orl right, then. Wot's the use o' wastin' yer time, goin' hin?'

'But there *might* be something.'

'Ah, then you'd be an idjit to go hin,' exclaimed Ben, triumphantly crowning his point. 'Get me?'

'I get you that you've no pluck,' she retorted, frowning.

'Ah, you orter seed me in the war, miss. I was blowed up by a mine once, and come dahn singin'.'

'Go on with you!' she said, trying to remain severe, and finding it rather difficult. He was a queer card. 'If that's true, go in *there* singing!'

She took hold of his arm, but he backed hastily away.

'That's dif'rent,' he frowned. 'We was orl together in the war like. But—wot's ter say there ain't a corpse in there?'

'Here—enough of that!' cried the woman.

'Lummy!' muttered Ben, following his new train of thought.

'I'll bet that's wot it is. A blinkin' corpse. That feller at the winder got in arter that Yank, the Yank murders 'im, and 'ops it.' Gentle perspiration moistened the theorist's brow as he added, '*Nah*, miss—'oo's goin' ter hopen that door?'

'I am,' responded the woman breathlessly.

Ben's theory terrified her, but it also decided her. The man in there might not be dead; he might be merely hurt, and require their aid. The utter silence of the inner room lent colour to these notions. Yes, yes—clearly, the door must be unlocked and opened without any more delay.

'Orl right—yer will 'ave it!' chattered Ben, as she turned the key. He looked round for a missile or weapon of some sort. A wooden chair was nearest, and he seized that. The door was flung open, and the woman entered.

Some breathless moments went by. She did not reappear.

'Oi!' shouted Ben, in a sudden frenzy. 'Oi!'

Raising his chair high, he approached the door, but sprang back as the woman suddenly reappeared.

'Lor' luvvaduck!' he gasped. 'Wotcher wanter spring at a feller like that for?'

'I wasn't springing—*you* did the spring,' she retorted, 'and if you're a specimen of the Merchant Service, then I'd sooner trust myself in a train!'

'Yer carn't do nothin' when ye'r' 'ungry,' growled Ben. 'Wotcher find in there?'

'Nothing.'

'Wot! Nothin' at all?'

'Nothing at all.'

Ben drank in this reassuring news. It put a new angle on things. He lowered his chair, and straightened his back—straightened it as far as it would straighten, that is. Then he said, impressively:

'You was too quick, you was, miss. You didn't give me no time, see? *I'm* a-goin' hin!'

He marched to the door, but even though he knew the room was empty, he hesitated for an instant on the brink. Almost pitch-dark, for the light that should have entered the window was practically fogged out, it looked a gloomy hole. He could just discern the outline of the table in the middle of the room, and of a chair that seemed to have been hastily shoved aside. Yes, a very gloomy hole—yet a palace of delight to another Ben was soon to enter.

'I thought you were going "hin"?' observed a sarcastic voice behind him.

'So I am goin' hin,' retorted Ben, 'but I ain't no hexpress trine!'

He entered cautiously. She had said the room was empty, but, after all, there might be somebody under the table, or behind that big arm-chair in the corner. He groped about, and suddenly, like a child anxious to get a nasty business over, he bent down and lifted an edge of the table-cloth. That he saw nothing was, at first, no proof that there was nothing to see, because in his terror lest he should see a pair of eyes staring out at him, he had instinctively closed his own eyes. But when he opened them, they met blankness, and he breathed again.

'Thank Gawd!' he murmured. 'This is a narsty bizziness, s'elp me it is!'

His mind relieved, he now proceeded to examine the room with elaborate thoroughness. If the Merchant Service had lagged behind a little, it would at least prove that, when it once tackled a job, it tackled it properly. Ben examined the table, noting the half-finished meal (which in other circumstances he would very promptly have finished), and then he looked behind all the chairs—yes, even the big ones with the backs you couldn't see round. He did take one curtain for granted, but he prodded the other one, and, as he did so, something slipped off the bottom of it.

''Allo—wot's this?' he queried.

He stooped and picked up the object. In the gloom he could hardly distinguish what it was, but it appeared to be a small cardboard ticket or badge. He struck a match. The light flared abruptly upon a number, written large upon the cardboard's surface.

'Seventeen,' muttered Ben, staring at it. 'Wot the 'ell's that mean? Number Seventeen!'

He dropped the match suddenly. Someone had entered the bar parlour from the road. He could hear the steps. Lummy!

Then he smiled.

'Idjut!' he thought. ''Er father come 'ome, o' course!'

He strode out of the room, making a brave show, and nearly fell into the arms of a policeman.

'Hallo!' exclaimed the policeman. 'Wot's this?'

For a moment, Ben was wordless—he never did feel really comfortable with policemen—and the woman explained.

'Oh, he's all right,' she said. 'Don't worry about him.

But I'm glad you've come—there's been funny goings on here, I can tell you.'

'Yes, that's *why* I've come,' answered the constable. 'This is pickpockets' weather, and I've seen some funny characters round about here.' He looked at Ben suspiciously. 'I ain't too sure this isn't one of 'em!'

''Oo? Me?' expostulated Ben indignantly. 'Well, if that ain't sorse! 'Ere I stays, ter proteck a gal, and now you comes along—'

'Steady, steady!' interposed the constable. 'There's funny people about, I tell you, and I've seen some of them about this place. One ran out of this inn just now, but I couldn't catch him.'

'Yes, there was something funny about him,' agreed the woman. 'He left in a hurry, without even finishing his meal.'

'And I expect this man would have left in a hurry too,' observed the constable, ironically. 'Open your hand! What have you got there?'

'Wot, this?' answered Ben. 'Picked it up in that room there jest now. 'Ere—don't snatch!'

The constable whipped the piece of cardboard out of Ben's hand.

'Hallo!' he exclaimed. 'What's this?'

'My age,' replied Ben.

'Now, then, don't be funny,' frowned the constable.

'Well, 'ow do I know wot it is,' retorted Ben. 'You ain't give me time to look yet. Got it off the floor—'

'Yes, so you say,' interposed the constable, and turned to the woman. 'Have you seen this before?'

'No, never.'

'He says he picked it off the floor in the next room.'

'Well, he may have done so.'

'Were you in the next room before him?'

'Yes, I was.'

'And *you* didn't see anything on the floor?'

'No. But it was dark. I didn't look everywhere. I expect it belonged to that other man.'

'Oh, you do? Well, that's got to be proved, and meanwhile it's on this man—'

'Yes, but what is it, anyway?' asked the woman, trying to get a peep at it.

'Something—mighty queer,' replied the constable darkly. 'Don't ask no questions, and you won't be told no lies. But I dare say our friend here—'

He turned to Ben. But Ben was gone. He had decided to forgo his Carlton luncheon.

3

Ben Finds His Port

Swallowed completely by the fog, for the first time Ben appreciated it. Perhaps he had left the inn more hurriedly than wisely, and the sacrifice of a good square meal certainly rankled in his hungry breast. But Ben liked a quiet life—he had only chosen the sea because it took him away from the land—and it had seemed to him that he had been caught up in a network of uncomfortable matters which were no concern of his, and for which he was in no way responsible. That being so, he argued that the best thing he could do was to cut quite clear of them, and to begin, so to speak, afresh.

The constable may have been talking through his hat, of course. He may have been saying more than he meant. But, contrariwise, he may have meant more than he said, and Ben did not see why he should take any chances. Particularly with a nice, comfortable, all-concealing fog just outside.

So into the fog he had slipped, and through it he now ran, in the innocent belief that his troubles were over.

He managed to steer an uninterrupted course for a full ten minutes, and then the person he bumped into was nothing more alarming than an elderly gentleman with a bad corn.

'Where are you going to?' barked the elderly gentleman.

'Sime spot as you was,' replied Ben, hunger and the fog rendering him something of a daredevil.

As he hurried on, he recalled the gleam of the elderly gentleman's gold watch-chain, and he wondered how many square meals that could have been converted into.

'It's a lucky thing fer gold watches,' he reflected, 'that me mother taught me ter say me prayers reg'lar!'

Presently, feeling secure, he slackened his pace; and indeed this was necessary, for although he could not see London, he felt it beginning to envelop him. Houses loomed up, when he hit one side of the road or the other. People became more frequent, and meetings ceased to be events, or bumpings to surprise. Traffic groped and hooted along the road, lamp-posts dawned—a mile away one moment and upon you the next—and, every now and again, voices were suddenly raised in warning, or anxiety, or irony.

The fog entered Ben's brain, as well as his eyes. Soon, he was walking in a sort of a trance. If you had stopped him and asked where he was walking, he could not have told you, and he might have had difficulty, also, in telling you why he walked—until, at any rate, he had had several seconds to consider the matter. He was travelling very much like a rudderless ship, borne by the tide into whatever port, or on to whatever rocks, that tide decreed.

But, at last, Ben's dormant will did assert itself for a brief instant, though even here Fate selected the particular restaurant into which he turned, to add another link to the strange chain that was binding him. It was, of course, a cheap restaurant, for an out-of-work seaman can patronise no other, and it was nearly empty. Ben shuffled to a pew-like seat with a high back, sat down, and ordered a cup of tea and as much bread-and-butter as would be covered by fourpence. Then he settled himself to his simple meal, comparing it regretfully with the more lavish repast he had missed earlier in the day.

He was seated near the end of the long, narrow room, and only one table lay beyond—a table completely hidden by the high back of his bench. He had vaguely imagined this end table to be unoccupied, but suddenly a word fell upon his ears, and he paused in the act of conveying a substantial piece of bread-and-butter to his mouth. For the word he had heard was 'Seventeen.'

'That's rum,' he thought. 'Seems as if I can't git away from the blinkin' number terday!'

He cocked his ears. Soon, another voice made a remark—a girl's voice this time. The first voice had been a man's.

'Isn't there any other way?' asked the girl's voice.

It was sullen and dissatisfied, and the man's voice replied somewhat tartly:

'What other way do you suggest?'

Apparently the girl made no response, for the man repeated his question, as though nervous and irritated.

'Oh, I don't care,' said the girl's voice, in accents suggesting the accompaniment of a shrug. 'It's all the same in the end.'

'That's where you're a fool!' rasped the man's voice. It was kept low, but Ben had no difficulty in hearing the words. 'It's not the same in the end. There's a hell of a difference!'

'To you, I dare say.'

'And to you, to. Why—' The remark was interrupted by the dull sound of a train. Evidently, there was a line running past the back of the shop. 'That's a bit funny, isn't it?' exclaimed the man's voice.

'What's funny?' demanded the girl's voice.

'Why—that train.'

'I can't see where the fun comes in.'

''Ear, 'ear,' thought Ben. 'Wot's funny in a trine—hexcep' when it's on time?'

The voices ceased, and the piece of bread-and-butter completed its postponed journey to Ben's mouth. While it was followed by another, and another, Ben tried to visualise the owners of the voices. It may be mentioned that he visualised them all wrong. The man developed in his mind like Charlie Peace, and the girl like Princess Mary.

He began to fall into a reverie, but all at once he cocked his ears again. The conversation behind him was being resumed.

'Well, well, we needn't decide this minute,' muttered the man, 'but the only thing I can see is Number Seventeen.'

'Blimy, and it's the on'y thing I can *'ear*,' thought Ben.

'I'll tell you what it is,' retorted the girl. 'You're getting nervy.'

'Nervy, is it?'

'Yes. Nothing's happened to worry about yet. Why, we've only just—'

'Quiet!' whispered the man fiercely. 'Haven't you got any sense at all?'

After a short silence, the girl's voice remarked, with irony:

'I haven't had much up till now. But it's coming.'

'A bit cryptic, aren't you, my girl?' observed the man.

'Then here's something else cryptic,' she answered. 'Why will some people persist in wearing blinkers?'

'Now we're goin' ter 'ave a little dust-up,' thought Ben. 'Two ter one on the gal!'

The dust-up did not materialise, however. Instead, a bulky form materialised, walking up the shop. It was the bulky form of a policeman, and the policeman entered Ben's pew, and sat down opposite him.

'Well, I'm blowed!' thought Ben. 'This is my lucky dye! Thank Gawd, the bobbies don't turn hup in seventeens!'

The policeman looked at Ben, and nodded.

'Pretty thick outside there, isn't it?' he remarked.

'Yus,' answered Ben.

'Worst fog I ever remember,' continued the policeman. 'Looks as if it's going to last a week.'

'Yus,' said Ben.

The policeman smiled. 'Putting something warm inside you, eh?'

'That's right.'

'Well, tea's better than beer.'

'No. I means, yus.'

'How would you like another cup?'

Ben began to grow suspicious. People were not usually kind to him unless they had some ulterior motive.

'No, thanks, guv'nor,' he mumbled, rising abruptly. 'I got an appointment.'

The policeman looked at him rather hard.

'Where are you going to sleep tonight?' he asked.

Out of the corner of his eye, Ben saw the waitress approaching.

''Aven't reely decided yet,' he answered. 'Is the Ritz any good?'

'Fourpence,' said the waitress.

While Ben forked out, the policeman seemed to be looking at him rather harder. In fact, he was so interested in Ben's pockets, that Ben turned them inside out.

'No deception, guv'nor,' he remarked. 'There goes the end of it.'

'Then it don't look much like the Ritz for you,' observed the policeman. 'But, of course, if you'd done a little post-office robbery today, now, you'd keep your notes in some other pocket, wouldn't you?' Ben stared at him, and the policeman laughed. 'Your face tells your story, mate, as well as your pockets,' he said. 'Here's a shilling for that bed at the Ritz.'

Ben began to readjust his ideas about the police force.

'Wot's this?' he asked. 'A catch?'

'That depends on you,' smiled the policeman, and tossed him the coin.

Ben caught it. It occurred to him that, if he stayed any longer, he might grow sentimental, or the policeman might want his shilling back. Both events would be pitiable. So, slipping the coin into his pocket, he murmured, 'Toff, guv'nor, yer are—stright!' and shuffled out of the shop.

Through the fog once more Ben resumed his strange way, drawing nearer and nearer every moment to the unseen port that was waiting for him. Warmed by the tea, and cheered by his unexpected affluence, he groped his way along while the short day began to slip unnoticed into evening. The death of the day was not marked by gathering darkness, but by a change in the texture of a darkness already present.

'Wunner wot it's orl abart?' reflected Ben. 'Fust that there ticket I picked up in that there pub—Number Seventeen—and then that there tork in that there restrong—Number Seventeen agin. And then them bobbies. And then that feller leavin' in the middle of 'is meal like that. And then that fice at the winder—Gawd, that give me the creeps, stright! And then those two quarrellin' quiet-like, and then that bobby torkin' ter me abart a post-orfice robbery, and then givin' me a shillin' becos' o' me angel-fice . . . It's rum, 'owever yer looks at it . . . 'Allo. Steady, there!'

He had swerved against a parapet, and as he collected himself and began to swerve away again, a faint, muffled sound rushed by on the other side of the wall.

'Trine,' thought Ben, and his mind harped back to the reference to the train in the restaurant. 'Wot's funny abart a trine?'

He swerved a little too far from the wall, and got off the pavement. A bus-driver shouted at him. He shouted back, and returned to the pavement. Progress grew more difficult. Instinctively, he groped about for some quiet district, where the traffic would be less and the expectation of life greater. He walked mechanically for ten minutes, or an hour, or two hours—he couldn't say which. And then, abruptly, a practical sense entered into him, he realised that he was tired, and that he needed a plan.

'This ain't no night fer the Embankment,' he pondered. 'Besides, 'ow'd one find the blinkin' Embankment?'

It would be a pity, too, to waste precious coppers in an apology for a bed—even if he could find that, either. Maybe, if he set seriously to work, he could discover some odd corner to curl into for the night, a corner that would cost him nothing and would allow him to wake up no poorer than he had been when he went to sleep. Somewhere round about here, perhaps. It was quiet enough. Not a sound came to him, not a movement. Even the fog itself hung heavy and static.

'Yus, I'll 'ave a look rahnd,' thought Ben, and suddenly stopped dead.

He was standing by a lamp-post, the light of which revealed dimly the lower portion of an empty house. The door of the house was ajar, and upon it was the number 'Seventeen.'

4

The Empty House

Ben stared at the number, closed his eyes, opened them again, and then emitted a simple but expressive exclamation.

'Well, I'll be blowed!' he gasped. 'There ain't no gettin' away from it!'

A queer sensation passed through him as he stood on the narrow strip of pavement that divided the lamp-post from the railings, and blinked at the number that had dogged him ever since he had entered the arena of fog. But, after all—why *should* he get away from it? The number had not hurt him yet. There were hundreds of houses numbered 'Seventeen.' And this house was an empty house, with the door ajar!

'Come in!' the door seemed to say. 'Here's your free lodging. I've been waiting for you!'

Ben hesitated, annoyed with himself for his hesitation. This was the very thing he had been looking for. A gift from the gods! Just because . . .

'G'arn!' he muttered to himself, and walked to the front steps.

Now he was on them—there were only four—and the half-open door was two feet in front of his nose. He turned his head, and glanced back into the fog. It was so thick that he could not see the railings he had passed through. The dim light from the lamp-post sent its feeble rays above them, appearing to have no object in the world but to tell a wayfaring seaman that this house was No. 17, and that he must not pass it by. It would hardly have surprised Ben if the lamp-post had suddenly gone out now, its mission done. It appeared to be waning from where he stood.

Satisfied that nobody was immediately behind him, Ben turned to the door again, crept up to it, and gave it a careful, gentle push. It yielded rather more easily than he had expected, and he prepared to spring back. But nothing jumped out at him. A dark, narrow passage was revealed, and the beginning of an ascending staircase.

Rounding upon himself once more for his fears, he entered; and as soon as he entered, his fears returned.

''Ow do I know there ain't nobody be'ind that door?' he thought.

Anxiously, he peeped. Nobody was hiding behind the door. The house was as silent as a tomb.

'Well, we'll keep the fog aht, any'ow,' muttered Ben, and closed the front door quickly.

That was better! Now no one could leap in from the street. To ensure further against this unpleasant possibility, Ben bolted the door, and then turned to other places where leaping creatures might lurk. It will have been noted, long before now, that Ben was not a man of iron; but even a man made of sterner stuff than Ben might be forgiven for a few qualms in a strange, empty house, with a thick fog outside, and no illumination inside.

To remedy the latter evil—temporarily—Ben struck a match.

'Oi!' he shouted, as something rose and jumped at him.

He dropped the match, and it went out. He lunged, and hit nothing. Whatever had jumped at him had not repeated the attack.

Trembling, he struck another match, holding it behind him ready to hurl at the oncomer. Something stood against the wall . . . His shadow.

'Oh, my Gawd!' chattered Ben, and gave himself ten seconds to recover.

A thought came to him. Until he was quite certain that the house was unoccupied, was it wise, after all, to have the front door bolted? A bolted door would militate against his speed if, by chance, he desired a sudden exit. Napoleon, working out the tactics of Waterloo, was no more earnestly absorbed than was Ben, working out the tactics of a bolted door.

'Yus, I better *hun*bolt it, I reckons,' he concluded, at last. 'Yus—that's the idea. *Hun*bolt it.'

So he unbolted the front door, suppressing a shiver as he did so, and then, striking another match, surveyed the passage in detail.

On his right was a door. A little farther along on the right, where the hall narrowed to accommodate the rickety stairway that ascended by the left wall, was another door. And opposite the second door was a gap, presumably leading down to the basement.

He approached the first door. 'Wot's wrong with knockin'?' he thought. He knocked. There was no response. Opening the door slowly, he inserted his head, holding his match about him. An empty, furnitureless room greeted his eyes. The match flickered out.

''Andsome dining-room,' he commented, 'with ceiling comin' dahn.'

Closing the door, he proceeded to the second door, farther along the passage, and repeated the operation. The result was similar, only this time it was a ''andsome drawing-room, with piper peelin' orf.' Having closed the drawing-room door, he turned and peered into the inky gap that led down to the basement.

'Oh, well—'ere goes!' he murmured. 'Sailors was made ter go dahn!'

He descended into the unpleasant abyss, and spent five more matches on it. They revealed the usual rooms one finds in a basement, bare and tenantless; but there was one door he could not open. It was a stout door, evidently locked, though his match went out before he could find the keyhole. Deciding not to waste any more matches—for they were growing precious—he felt about in the darkness, even running his fingers along the bottom of the door.

'Cupboard, I hexpeck,' he muttered. 'But it's got a 'ell of a draught!'

The next moment, he bounded back. Something was happening beneath him. The floor was vibrating, and a faint, rhythmic clack came to his ears. Then, suddenly, the vibration increased, a dull roar grew out of the bowels of the earth, and something rushed beneath him. Ben wiped his damp forehead.

'If I 'ad the bloke 'ere,' he thought, 'wot hinvented trines, *I'd* give 'im somethin'.'

He ascended from the basement to the ground floor. He walked to the foot of the stairs leading to the upper floors. He raised his eyes, and peered, and listened.

And, as he listened, it began to dawn upon Ben that he

had done about as much exploring as his nerves would stand. Why go over the entire house? He wasn't bringing a whole family in! One floor was sufficient for him, and the drawing-room with the paper peeling off was quite good enough for his unfastidious taste.

So he sent his voice upstairs, instead of his person.

'Oi!' he shouted. 'Oi! Hennybody hup there?'

Apparently not. Still, he tried again.

'If hennybody's hup there,' he called, 'this is ter let 'em know as I'm dahn 'ere!'

Again no response. Ben sighed with relief.

'Well, it ain't so bad,' he observed, to the unheeding walls. 'I reckons this is a little bit of orl right! I'm a bloomin' 'ouse-holder. And nah, wot abart goin' aht and gettin' a bit o' food?'

He went to the front door, and opened it. Fog poured in. 'Lummy!' he thought. 'It's gettin' wuss!' Wedging a piece of wood, of which there was plenty about, under the door to keep it open, he walked down the steps and into the street again. And, just as he reached the pavement, the door of the adjoining house opened, and a figure emerged.

'Don't be long, father!' cried someone, evidently standing in the hall.

'I'll be as quick as I can, my dear,' the figure answered. 'Run in, or you'll catch your death of cold.'

The door closed with a muffled bang, and Ben drew himself close against the railings. The figure reached him abruptly, and paused in passing.

'Hallo—where did you spring from?' asked the figure.

Ben made no reply. He did not see why he should. A fellow didn't have to explain himself to every passer-by, did he, even if he *had* just been exploring an empty house that wasn't his! The figure looked at him suspiciously, and barked:

'Be off!'

And then, without waiting to find out whether this somewhat peremptory order was obeyed, went off himself.

A few seconds later, the front door of the next house again opened. Quickly, this time, as though on urgent business.

'Father!' called the voice he had heard before. 'Father! I want you to . . .'

There was no response, and the voice trailed off.

'Like me ter go arter 'im, miss?' asked Ben. 'Oi!'

The girl started at Ben's voice, and he slipped after the vanished figure. The fog beat him, however. He returned a minute later to report failure.

'Sorry, miss,' he said. ''E was too quick fer me. It's a reg'ler needle in a 'aystack in this fog, ain't it?'

'Never mind,' replied the girl. 'Thanks very much. It doesn't matter.'

She was a pretty girl, with nothing swanky about her. Quite a good sort, Ben concluded. Ripe for a little human intercourse, he attempted to prolong the conversation.

'Anythin' I can do for yer, miss?' he asked.

She peered down at him, and shook her head.

'No, thank you,' she said. 'It wasn't important—only a letter.'

'Like me ter post it?'

'No—but thank you very much.'

The door began to close. Ben felt as though a glint of sunlight had suddenly appeared, and were now vanishing.

'Shockin' dye, ain't it!' he called. The door, however, was now shut. 'Well, that's orl there is abart that!' he mumbled. 'That's the larst I'll see of '*er*!'

An extraordinarily poor prediction, as subsequent events proved. And had Ben realised the conditions of their next meeting, he would have sat down very promptly in the middle of the road.

Alone once more, he took careful bearings, and felt his way along the street, his idea being to keep a straight line until he hit a shop. He did not hit a shop until he had crossed three roads, and then it was not much of a shop. True, it called itself an Emporium, in virtue of the fact that the old lady who kept it had blossomed out from sweets to postcards and a small selection of tinned foods; but the sweets and the post-cards were of modest quality, while the tinned foods were reduced to the single selection of pork and beans.

''Ow much?' demanded Ben, taking up the single selection.

'One-and-two, or one-and-three, I think,' replied the old lady. 'Dear me, I must get some more.'

'Let it go fer a shillin', ma?' asked Ben.

'We'll say one-and-two, then.'

'But I ain't got one-and-two. I got a shillin'.'

She looked at him, over her glasses. He was very shabby. And it was very foggy. And she was very old. Details don't matter quite so much when you are old.

'All right, then—a shilling,' she said; and the bargain was struck.

He groped his way back to the empty house, noted with satisfaction that the door was as he had left it, and slipped in with his precious packet. This time, he bolted the front door behind him and, after depositing his parcel in the back reception-room, he descended to the basement to make certain that the back door was bolted also. This settled, he returned to the back reception-room, and prepared to make himself comfortable.

He tested the floor by sitting down in a corner of it. Not at all bad. Quite decent, in fact. So decent, that he had no immediate impulse to get up again. Of course, he'd get up soon. He'd find some wood and make a fire. Then, a little later, he would heat the pork and beans on the fire . . . that would be good . . . but not just yet . . . a little later . . .

He began to nod. His head drooped forward. Ben had walked a good many miles that day. A clock outside chimed six.

Ben did not hear it—he was fast asleep.

He awoke suddenly, with a start. The clock was striking again—midnight. But that had not awakened him. Someone was walking in the basement below.

5

Up and Down

'G'arn—I'm dreamin',' thought Ben. 'Orl them doors is bolted!'

He stayed quite still, listening, and hoping to be awakened from the dream. But the footsteps continued, and grew louder, and all at once Ben realised that this was no dream, but stark reality. The knowledge produced a frank sweat.

The moment when the dream theory fails is always a nasty one.

'S'elp me, there's a bloke dahn there,' gasped Ben, and clambered clumsily to his feet.

Then he stood motionless, and listened again. Now he heard no sound. The footsteps had stopped. Was the producer of the footsteps also listening, standing somewhere below as motionless as he?

Ben crept to the door, and softly opened it. As he did so, a dull clank-clank in the distance grew nearer and louder. A goods train, obviously. It rattled under the house, shaking it, and under cover of the noise Ben left the room and stepped out into the passage.

'P'r'aps it was the trine, orl the time,' thought Ben, as the rattle and clank decreased.

But this hope was soon dissipated. Even before the sound of the train had dwindled away, the footsteps below recommenced—less heavily, this time more stealthily.

''Ere, I've 'ad enuff o' this!' reflected the seaman, and tiptoed quickly along the passage.

Should he dash out of the house? This would mean unbolting the front door—a noisy operation—and it would also mean the rest of the night in the fog. A speedier, and probably better, sanctuary was suggested by the staircase. Almost before he realised it, he was ascending the stairs, and he did not pause in his ascent until he had reached the top of the house.

He found himself now on a small landing with a skylight above him, and a door on his right. There was only one door, leading assumedly to an attic.

Before entering the door, he turned and peered down the stairs up which he had come. All was quiet. He waited, so it seemed to him, five minutes, but probably it was only one. Then he turned to the attic door again, and regarded it.

Risking the sound, he struck a match. A key was in the door, and this immediately suggested his plan. He stretched his hand forward, and turned the key. The door was now locked, with the initiative on his side, and he was free to negotiate.

'Oi!' he whispered, through the keyhole. 'Hennybody there?'

No answer came. He repeated the inquiry, a little more loudly, but not too loudly, lest the thing below stairs should hear. Then, as again no answer came, and as he heard neither breathing nor snoring, he felt free to turn the key, and open the door.

Another match revealed the chamber, and proved that, although less pretentious from the architect's point of view, it had certain advantages over the lower rooms he had already sampled. The first advantage was a half-used candle, sticking upright in a pool of its own grease on the mantelpiece across the floor. Ben made for the candle promptly, and by its comparatively brilliant glare noted the other advantages of the attic.

An old chair, battered but still serviceable, was near the fireplace. Three or four packing-cases, which could be used as tables or firewood, stood about. And the key in the door was another advantage, for it offered security.

But before Ben could finally approve of the room, two other doors had to be investigated.

One door, by the fireplace, led to an inner room somewhat similar to the outer room. Rendered courageous by his candle, he made a thorough examination of this inner chamber, discovering that it possessed no other entrance, and that it contained a fair-sized cupboard.

The other door of the outer room, at right angles to the passage door, and close to it, refused to open. It was locked—as the door down in the basement had been—and there was no key.

'This is a better pitch,' thought Ben. 'I'll stay 'ere till the mornin', any'ow, and the feller dahnstairs can 'ave the bottom 'arf. Sort o' maisonette.'

Some packing-cases stood under a rather high window. He climbed on to them, and peered out. Fog still as thick as ever. Climbing down again, he selected the most dilapidated case, and split it up.

'Might as well 'ave a bit o' cheer,' he muttered. 'And it's time, I reckons, fer them pork an' beans.'

Fortunately, there were some odd scraps of paper in the packing-case, and these served to start the fire. Throwing some wood on top, he soon had a good blaze, and the warmth welled into him, making life good once more, and dispelling some of his tremors. Thus many another has enjoyed the calm before the storm, smiling for a short period in the false assurance of a temporary security.

His good humour increased when he opened the packet which contained the tin of pork and beans. The old proprietress of the Emporium had added a chunk of bread and a slice of cheese. Best bob's-worth he'd ever known. This was a bit of all right!

'Me own mother wouldn't 'ave done more fer me,' thought Ben. 'Wot it is ter 'ave a 'andsome fice!'

But, although he made light of it, the old woman's kindliness warmed that bare, uncomfortable room almost as much as did the crackling blaze. In the midst of all this uncouthness and uncanniness, of fearful possibilities and tremulous thoughts, a peaceful, human smile lurked somewhere. It stood for the tiny gleam that no blackness can ever totally extinguish, though often enough we seem to lose it in our groping, and forget that it is there. Yet, however faintly it burns, it never flickers out, for it is independent of material substance.

He had some difficulty in opening the tin, and might have been reduced to stamping upon it but for a nail which he wrenched from one of the packing-cases. Putting the tin carefully on the fire, he watched its congealed contents soften and warm, munching bread and cheese to assuage his impatience. He had no spoon, so he stirred the pork and beans with his finger, to help them on their way, and also for the pleasure of sucking his finger afterwards. The operation was so successful that he stirred the pork and beans several times, until they got too hot for the process. Then, to ensure peace with his meal, he tiptoed out on to the landing once more, and listened.

A blessed silence greeted him.

A faint noise in the room he had just left, however, disturbed the blessedness. His mind instantly flashed to the locked door, and he visualised it slowly opening, and heaven knows what coming out! Had he stopped to think, he might have fled downstairs, but the two things he loved best in all the world were in that room—the pork and beans and the candle—and they were worth some risk in this house of risks. He returned to the room rapidly, and disturbed a little mouse enjoying a crumb of cheese.

''Ere—wotcher mean, pretendin' ter be a ghost?' demanded Ben indignantly.

The mouse, like Ben, became divided against itself. This great, hulking thing was a terror; but the cheese was wonderfully succulent. Two reproachful eyes peered up at Ben from the boards.

'Oh, go hon—don't mind me!' jeered Ben. 'But, look 'ere, Charlie, you was 'ere while I was gorn—didjer see that there door a-movin' jest nah?'

He jerked his thumb towards the locked door. The mouse, still eyeing him solemnly, refused to commit itself.

'Boo!' cried Ben.

A frenzied flash, and the mouse was gone. Ben felt no animosity against the mouse, but it gave him a sort of satisfactory feeling to frighten something. Moreover, it suggested a pleasant theory. If he could scare a mouse, without any desire to harm the mouse, why could not something scare Ben, without any desire to harm Ben?

This thought was rudely disturbed by a new emotion. The tin on the fire slipped, and began to pour itself out.

'Oi!' gasped Ben. ''Arf a mo'!'

He rushed across, and rescued the tin, nearly scalding his hand in the process. Luckily, not more than a penn'orth had flowed away.

Many strange things were destined to happen in this room within the next twenty-four hours, and while Ben is busy with his pork and beans, it may be as well for us to examine the room a little more closely. Its walls and ceiling were in a most dilapidated condition. The paper was yellow with age, and in some places had peeled right off. In others, it was peeling. Here and there, bits of the ceiling had come down, and the vibration caused by the trains that ran under the house suggested one cause of this. The trains could still be heard from the attic, though the sound was naturally fainter and more muffled than it had been down in the basement.

Facing the door by which Ben had entered the room, and with our back to the opposite blank wall, we note two or three packing-cases that lined the left-hand wall, ceasing at the locked door which Ben had not been able to open. This locked door was near the corner of the room, and round the corner came the door to the passage—a small passage containing, in addition to the attic door, nothing more notable than the head of the descending staircase, and above, in the low roof, the skylight. Inside the room again, to the right of the passage door as one turned and faced it, were more packing-cases. By climbing upon them one could reach a small, high window, which Ben had noted with satisfaction was closed. Then, round the corner to the next right-hand wall, came a bare space, the door leading to the inner chamber, the fireplace, and the single, battered chair.

Such was the configuration and furnishing of this room of destiny, where an out-of-work seaman sat dispatching pork and beans.

His simple meal over, Ben smiled contentedly, and prepared once more to make himself comfortable for the night—or, for the rest of the night. Towards this end, he poked his head into the inner chamber, assuring himself again that it was empty, and made one last effort to get the locked door on the opposite wall open. Failure, of course, greeted this effort. Finally, he stepped out on to the little landing . . .

'Ah, not this time, lovey!' he chuckled, as a soft sound came to him—not from below. 'I ain't feared o' mice no more!'

The soft sound continued, and he tiptoed back to the room to give his little friend another surprise. But no small eyes greeted him this time. Nor was there any flashing scurry. His grin froze on his face, as he realised that, this time, a mouse was not responsible.

Ben had not gained a reputation for speed in the Merchant Service, but there were times when he acted quickly. This new soft sound was worse than anything he had heard—he could not define it, or place it. But it was up here—somewhere—which meant that Ben must get down there, anywhere, He scampered down the stairs like a frightened rat.

But, even in that mad scamper, he stopped dead at the head of the stairs that led down to the ground floor. Someone was below, with footsteps as hurrying as Ben's.

And the footsteps were coming up.

6

Under the Lamp-Post

The fog did not lift through the night. London awoke to another day of yellowness, the optimists rubbing their eyes, the pessimists croaking. More blind groping, more wheezing and coughing, and more traffic strangulation. Only the companies that profited by artificial illumination, and the children who profited by the absence of their governess, smiled as they greeted the opaque morning. The rest of the world saw small joy in the adventure.

All day long, the ineffective lamp-post outside the house of strange happenings flickered intermittently upon the number, '17,' Often, the number could not be read at all, despite the nearness of the light, but sometimes the fog thinned a little, and then the number grew out and vaguely beckoned. But few of the few people who passed along that unfrequented road troubled to notice it. Why should they? And, certainly, no one thought of answering its grim invitation.

A fog is bad enough. Who wants an empty house thrown in?

Between three and four in the afternoon, however, a passer-by might have paused. The house was dark and silent, saving for a very faint flicker in the top room. This flicker suddenly disappeared, to reappear a few seconds afterwards behind a window on the lower floor. Then, again, it vanished, and then again it appeared on the ground floor. After that, it vanished completely.

And then a passer-by did indeed come along, and appear to respond to the house's grim invitation. He was a man with a crooked shoulder, and he paused outside the house and looked at it. As though to ensure his interest, the fog thinned momentarily, allowing the street lamp to shine more clearly on the number '17,' and even revealing, for an instant, the front door.

The front door was ajar.

The man with the crooked shoulder looked at the door; then, turning his head, he glanced up and down the street. His eyes, of course, met nothing, since another man could have been standing five feet off without being seen. When he turned his head back to the front door, the fog had thickened again and he could no longer see the door. But he knew the door was ajar, and the knowledge fascinated him.

He stood there, perhaps, twenty seconds. Then, suddenly, he slipped into the house, and the door closed behind him.

And now it really seemed as though that silent street of ghosts and whisperings began to wake up and enter the arena of more normal, commonplace matters. A new figure groped its way along the pavement, a figure, this time unsinister and fashionable.

'Hey! W-where are you?' it stammered. 'Where the d-dickens—'

It turned, and looked back—or tried to look back—along the way it had come. A well-dressed young man, with a good-natured, pleasant face, was revealed by the lamp-light. The lamp-post itself was revealed to the young man only when he backed into it.

'Hallo! So *there* you are!' he cried, in a voice of relief. 'Where the devil did you g-get to, old chap? I—'

He stopped abruptly, as he turned to the lamp-post. Good-humoured annoyance shone on his features.

'Oh! It's you, is it?' he exclaimed. 'Well, h-haven't you got something b-better to do than to stand there pretending to be a h-h-human being?'

He brushed himself, then raised his voice and called into the callous mist.

'Fordyce! FORDYCE! Where the devil *are* you?' He strained his ears for a reply, but none came. 'Oh, all right—I don't care!' he ran on. 'But just tell me this. W-what's the b-bally use of a f-feller who meets a f-feller and can't stick to a f-feller in a f-fog?'

No one answered the question. He veered round, shook his fist at the lamp-post, and then leaned against it. In his depressing circumstances, no little bit of comfort the street offered could be neglected.

'What weather!' he muttered. 'Lovely! Sunshine in L-London, thirteen hours decimal eight. I don't think. Je ne pense pas. Ich glaube nicht. And in all the other b-bally languages! . . . I s'pose this *is* London? Upon my soul, it m-might be Timbuctoo for all one can s-see of it.'

He waited a minute, then raised his voice and called again.

'Fordyce! Fordyce! Gilbert Fordyce! Fordyce Gilbert! B-biggest ass that ever was, is, or w-will be, where *are* you?' He began to cough suddenly. 'There, that's done it! Broken my beastly larynx now. Well, I'll say this for you, old m-man. You may be a damned fool and s-stutter—yes, some p-people say you d-do stutter—but you've got the temper of a bally saint. H-haven't I, my long friend?' He gave the lamp-post a friendly, familiar slap. 'I say, you don't mind my talking to you, do you, old chap? Thanks, very much. Most awfully obliged. Even a lamp-post's company—when there ain't n-nobody else.'

As though in response, and to show what good company it could be, the light made an extra effort, and illuminated the number on the door-post. The young man stared at the number, and blinked. 'No. 17, eh? Sweet seventeen! Made a lot of m-money on you once at dear old Monte Carlo. Good old seventeen—hallo! W-who . . .'

The front door swung open suddenly, and a figure hurried out. It was the figure of a man with a crooked shoulder. He seemed in a considerable hurry, for he blundered down the steps and was into the young man before he knew it. The young man fell back against the lamp-post.

'What the hell—!' muttered the blunderer.

'Eh? Oh, don't mention!' replied the young man. 'I like it!'

The next moment he was alone again. The other had vanished. The young man stared into the void.

'Hi! W-wait a minute!' he cried, waking up. suddenly. 'W-what's the hurry? I'm not c-contagious! Hi!'

He ran after him, and the road was empty once more. And, almost as though it had waited until there were no observers, the light in the house which had descended from the top now reappeared, and began to ascend again. It flickered dimly behind windows of the ground floor and first floor. Soon, it reached the top floor. Then, all at once, it went out . . .

'Eddie!' called a voice, along the street. 'Eddie! Where are you?'

A tall, strong-limbed young man felt his way up to the lamp-post. He had come from the same direction as the stutterer, and was in the same predicament. But he did not expend his emotion upon the unresponsive lamp-post. Instead, he paused when he came to it, muttered, 'Damn!' and lit a cigarette.

And as he did so, the door of 'No. 17' burst open, and a terrified figure came flying out.

'Hello—what's all the excitement?' exclaimed Gilbert Fordyce, catching hold of the flying man's collar.

'Gawd!' choked the terrified figure, and hung limp in his captor's grasp.

7

Ben Tells His Story

Fordyce regarded with sympathy the sorry specimen of humanity hanging limply on his arm, but he did not allow that sympathy to affect his actions or his judgment. Here was some matter, clearly, which required careful investigation, so he tightened his grasp—for many a rascal 'acts floppy' before a frantic attempt to escape—and shook his captive gently.

'Now, then,' he repeated, 'what's all the excitement? Come along!'

His captive made no movement, and Fordyce concluded that he was not shamming. Still, he did not loosen his grip.

'Pull yourself together!' he urged, with another shake. 'Wake up!' He called again more sharply, 'Wake *up*!'

''Elp!' bellowed the man, suddenly obeying his captor's injunction, and waking up. He woke up so effectively that he began to struggle.

'Whoa! Steady!' reproved Fordyce. 'Don't be a fool! What's the matter?'

'Lemme go!'

'Certainly—when you've explained your hurry.'

''Urry,' chattered the limp figure. 'Gawd! You'd be in a 'urry if yer'd seed a corpse!'

Fordyce frowned, and studied the man a little more intently.

'Corpse, eh?' he said seriously. 'So you've seen a corpse?'

'Yes,' whined the man. 'Lemme go, guv'nor. I ain't done it! I ain't done it.'

'By Jove, this is serious. I—whoa! Whoa!' For the man had begun to struggle again. 'Steady, there! One mustn't run away from corpses, you know—it looks suspicious. Tell me some more about this corpse.' The man stopped struggling, and stared stupidly. Fordyce realised that whatever story lay behind the fellow's terror could only be elicited by patient cross-examination. 'Do you live in that house?' he asked quietly.

The man shivered.

'Wot—*me*? Live there?' he answered. '*Live* there? Lummy, no!'

'Ah. You don't?'

'Nah!'

'Sort of—lodger, eh?'

The man shook his head.

'It's a hempty 'ouse, guv'nor, see? Hempty 'ouse.'

'Oh, empty?'

'Yus.'

'Well, then,' proceeded Fordyce, 'if it's empty, what were *you* doing there? Come along! What were *you* doing in this empty house?'

'No 'arm, guv'nor, s'elp me!' mumbled the man.

'I didn't say—'

'Got in yesterday, guv'nor, ter git a bit o' shelter, see? Didn't mean no 'arm, guv'nor. Out o' work, see?'

Fordyce nodded, and now he let the man go, but he watched him narrowly for tricks.

'I see,' he said gently. 'Poor devil!'

'That's right, sir,' exclaimed the man eagerly, somewhat reassured by the other's attitude. 'Poor's right. Lorst me ship, guv'nor, and no fault o' me own. Ain't got no money. Ah, but I never murdered 'im! No, sir, I ain't that sort, s'elp me, I ain't!'

'Who says you murdered him?' retorted Fordyce, frowning. 'If you say that any more I'll begin to think you really have! Let's get on with this. You're an out-of-work sailor, I take it—'

'That's right. Merchant Service.'

'Good. It's noted. And you say that house is empty?'

'That's right. Hempty as my grave.'

'Charming simile!'

'Wot's that?'

'Never mind. Who's in there now?'

'Nah?' said the seaman, staring stupidly. 'Wot—nah?'

'Yes, now,' replied Fordyce sharply. 'At this moment.'

'Only—'im,' muttered the seaman, with a shudder.

''Im? Oh, the corpse.' An idea suddenly occurred to Fordyce. 'Tell me, do you drink?'

'Yus. No!'

'Quite a Parliamentarian,' observed Fordyce dryly. 'What does that mean, exactly?'

'Ain't 'ad a drop,' answered the seaman.

'Honour bright?'

'Ain't 'ad a charnce!'

'All right, I'll take your word for it,' smiled Fordyce. 'Like a drop now?'

The sailor's eyes popped. He eagerly seized the flask that was held out to him, and put it to his lips. When he judged the right moment had come, Fordyce took the flask away from him gently but firmly, and then proceeded with the cross-examination.

'Now get on with your story, and be quick about it,' he said. 'Then we'll have a look round—'

'Wot—go hin?' exclaimed the seaman, pausing in the act of wiping his mouth with the back of his hand.

'Yes, of course.'

The seaman shook his head very decidedly.

'I ain't goin' back into that 'ouse, guv'nor,' he observed, 'and doncher think it!'

'I'm afraid you'll have to,' returned Fordyce grimly, and seized the man's collar again swiftly. He was only just in time. 'Now, understand me once and for all, old son,' he remarked, with quiet assurance. 'It isn't likely that I'm going to pass this house, after what you've told me, without going in. And it isn't likely that I'll relieve myself of your company until I *have* gone in. Struggling's no use. No earthly. Have you got that? Don't be a fool, and act like a criminal before anyone accuses you!'

'I tells yer, stright, I ain't goin' back inter that 'ouse,' muttered the seaman miserably. 'It's give me the fair creeps, it 'as.'

'Creeps, eh? Well, of course, a corpse isn't exactly lively company.'

'Ah, but it wasn't the corpse wot started it,' explained the seaman sepulchrally. 'I got the creeps afore that. When fust I gits in the 'ouse, sir, there ain't nobody helse in the blinkin' plice, see? S'elp me, there wasn't. I goes hover the 'ole plice—leastwise, most of it—and there ain't nobody. But, afterwards—I 'eard things. Gawd, I 'eard things!'

'Why did you stay, if you were frightened?'

'Blimy if I knows, guv'nor,' answered the seaman, scratching his forehead. 'It was a roof, see? I 'adn't nowhere helse pertickler ter go. One plice is as good as another, when yer ain't got nowhere helse. And then, the fog, see? Thort I'd stick it fer a bit.'

'Yes, I see. Well, go on. About this corpse. No, wait a minute—tell me this, first. How did you get into the house?'

'Fahnd the door hopen.'

'Perhaps you didn't close it after you?' suggested Fordyce.

'Didn't I?' retorted the seaman. 'You can lay I did.'

'All right, then. I'll lay it. But someone might have let himself in with a latch-key after you, mightn't he?'

'No, 'e mightn't. 'E couldn't. I bolted the door.'

'What about the back door?'

'Bolted that, too.'

'I see,' nodded Fordyce, smiling faintly. 'You didn't want any surprise visitors. H'm. Well—why not?' The seaman did not reply, and Fordyce repeated his question more sharply. 'Why not? Done anything shady?'

''Ow many more times 'ave I got ter tell yer?' grumbled the seaman. 'I ain't done nothin' shidy! But—well, I didn't want people pokin' rahnd, see? 'Ouse wasn't mine.'

'Oh, quite so. You thought the rent collector might come along. So you closed all the doors and bolted them. Did you have to unbolt the front door just now, to get out?'

'Yus, sir. No, sir!'

'Yes, sir? No, sir? You can't have 'em both. Which'll you choose?'

The seaman reflected. His face bore a slightly puzzled look, as though he himself were as interested in this question as his interrogator.

'No, sir,' he said, after a pause. 'I *didn't* unbolt the door jest nah—'

'How was that?'

'I'm tellin' yer! I'm *thinkin*'! Lummy, give a bloke a charnst! I bin aht fer a bit, see, an' I hexpeck I fergot ter close it proper when I come hin—'

'What did you go out for?'

A flicker of indignation entered the seaman's eyes.

'Ter pick buttercups and daisies,' he said.

'Don't be funny.'

'Funny! Yer think *ye'r* funny, doncher? Wot did I go hout for? If yer was henny good at questions, yer'd hask, "Wot did I stop *hin* for?"'

'Yes, yes, but you've told me that,' replied Fordyce patiently. 'You said you'd got nowhere else to go. What I want to know now is why you went *out*—'

'Orl right, orl right! Went aht to try an' git a bit o' grub. 'Aven't 'ad nothin' orl day. Gawd, I've got a 'ole in me! But I didn't 'ave no luck. So I comes back, see, and I reckons I fergets ter shut that there door proper.' He reflected again on this theory. 'Yus. But—see 'ere, guv'nor—orl them doors was shut an' bolted in the night, they was, when I 'eard steps, that I'll swear to! Dahn at the bottom, they was.'

'And where were you?'

'Hup at the top,' answered the seaman obviously. 'Ah, but that was arter. Yus, that's where I was *arter*. Fust I was at the bottom. It was *arter* I went hup ter the top—'

'*Arter* what?' barked Fordyce, for the man was beginning to ramble badly. 'Keep your head!'

'Arter I 'eard them steps. Creepin' steps! Creepin'! That was in the night, guv'nor, see? But jest nah I thinks I 'ears 'em agin. Lord love us! I listens, see? Then I 'ears nothin'. Then I stops listenin', see? Then I 'ears 'em again. Steps, sir—creepin' steps—'

'Yes, yes, I can guess what they sounded like,' broke in Fordyce impatiently. 'Go on, go on! Where were you then—just now, you know?'

'Top room, sir, as I sed. Moved hup in the night.'

'Why?'

''Cos the noises was at the bottom.'

'Oh, yes, of course,' nodded Fordyce, stifling another smile. 'Stout feller! And were *these* noises at the bottom, too?'

'No. They was at the top.'

'I see. So then you moved down again?'

'G'arn!' retorted the seaman, with another flicker of spirit. 'Yus, I come dahn. And so'd hennybody! So'd *you*. I come dahn, and then nex' thing, I 'ears noises below—'

'And then you went up again?'

'I ain't no bloomin' 'ero, sir,' muttered the seaman. 'I went hup. I was fair frightened. Hup I goes, ter the top, and, when I gits there—that's where I sees it.' He covered his face with his grubby hands suddenly. 'Oh, Gawd! I ain't goin' back there, guv'nor—not agin I aint!'

He looked a miserable object, and Fordyce regarded him pityingly. He could not quite get the hang of the story, but one thing was obvious—the seaman had spent a most unpleasant night, and had every reason for his abhorrence of 'No. 17.' Once more, however, Fordyce refused to allow his sympathy to cloud his judgment. Anticipating rebellion, he again took hold of the man's arm, as he replied, briskly:

'I'm sorry, but I'm afraid there's no help for it. You'll

have to go back—only this time you can console yourself that you'll have me with you. Come along! We've wasted quite enough time as it is.'

'Lemme go!' shouted the seaman.

'Nothing doing.'

'Lemme go, I ses! It ain't nothin' ter do with me. I needn't 'ave told yer—'

'No, you needn't,' agreed Fordyce grimly. 'But you did. It's no good pulling, my man. Not the slightest. Come *on*!'

The seaman realised that it was no good pulling. He tried whining. His morale was at its very lowest ebb.

'Wot's yer gime?' he pleaded.

'My game is quite simple,' answered Fordyce. 'I want to have a look at that corpse of yours. Then, when I've seen it—if it's really there—we'll decide what's best to do.'

'I can tell yer that right nah, guv'nor,' interposed the seaman eagerly. 'Git a bobby!'

Fordyce laughed.

'You mean, *I* get a bobby,' he observed, 'while *you* beat a strategic retreat! No, thanks. Besides, how do you propose to find a bobby in this fog? I've spent ten minutes before now trying to find one in the bright sunlight. And then, there's another thing, my man,' he added, looking towards the door of the empty house. 'I want to be quite sure there *is* a corpse before I invite anybody else to look at it. Come—stir yourself. No, wait a bit.' He raised his voice, and called, 'Eddie! Eddie!'

'Gawd, is there another of yer?' muttered the unhappy seaman.

'Eddie! Ahoy, there! Eddie!' shouted Fordyce again. The fog choked the sound. He shrugged his shoulders. 'No good. Well, that's that.'

He gave the seaman a little shake.

''Ere—'arf a mo',' chattered the seaman.

Fordyce looked at him, and suddenly exclaimed:

'Yes, on second thoughts, half a mo' you shall have. I say, can I trust you to stand by for a second or two, while I write something?'

'Yus,' answered the seaman, a little too promptly. 'Wot's it goin' ter be, guv'nor? Yer will?'

'Pick up your cap,' laughed Fordyce, as he let the man's arm go. 'It's on the ground.'

The seaman stooped to retain his battered headgear, and as he did so, Gilbert Fordyce suddenly sat upon him.

'Oi!' bawled the seaman.

'Sorry,' replied the voice above him. 'I'm afraid I really can't trust you, old sport. Keep still.'

'Wotcher doin' of?' cried the outraged fellow. 'There's a dirty trick! It's a disgrice ter the Merchant Service, that's wot it is—'

'Be quiet!'

'It's a disgrice! I'll write ter the White Star line, I will. Tork abart bein' the hunder dog!' But the figure above refused to budge, and the figure below had little stamina to support his righteous indignation. 'Wot's yer gime?' he complained helplessly. 'Blimy if you ain't wors'n them footsteps! Wot's that ye'r' writin'?'

'I'll read it out, if you like,' responded Fordyce amiably. 'Only *do* stop wriggling!' He had taken a piece of paper out of his pocket, and was now busily scribbling.

'Wriggle yerself,' growled the seaman. 'It ain't heasy ter be a 'uman writin'-desk an' keep steady when yer ain't 'ad no practice.'

'Oh, shut up! Listen, if you're curious.' Fordyce read:

'"To Eddie Scott, or to any other interested party. A blind man once went into a dark room to look for a black cat that wasn't there"—'

''E's potty,' murmured the seaman.

'—"I am now in No. 17, looking for a corpse. If the hunt appeals to you, come right in. G. F." There—that satisfy you?'

He got off the man's back, and looked round for a place to deposit the paper. The seaman inquired, as he straightened himself:

'Wot's "G. F." stand for, guv'nor?'

'Oh, whatever you like,' answered Fordyce. 'Good fellow, great fun, generous foe—'

'Or giddy fool!' added the seaman.

'Capital!' laughed Fordyce. 'Excellent. Now that I know you've got a sense of humour, we shall get along ever so much better. Now, where can I put—ah! The very thing!' He took off his Homburg hat, rolled the paper up into a thin slip, stuck it in the hat-band, and hung the hat on one of the railing spikes. 'There, that'll do beautifully. And now, my friend—over the top! Or, rather up to the top!'

The sailor stared at the house. Terror returned to his eyes.

'Fer the larst time, guv'nor—' he pleaded.

Fordyce replied by taking hold of his arm again.

'Eyes front,' he said.

'Well,' mumbled the seaman, 'don't say arterwards as I didn't warn yer—'

'Quick march!'

'Gawd!' chattered the seaman; and they entered the house.

8

On the Stairs

'Whew!' murmured Gilbert Fordyce, as they entered the hall. 'What a gloomy hole!'

''Corse it's a gloomy 'ole,' mumbled his companion. 'Wotcher hexpeck? Pally der Dance?'

Fordyce paused, and looked along the hall. The seaman followed his gaze, and shifted his feet uncomfortably.

'See anythin'?' he asked.

'No,' answered Fordyce slowly. 'But I was just wondering whether we oughtn't—'

'There—don't yer 'ear that?' chattered the seaman suddenly.

'No, I don't hear anything,' replied Fordyce. 'But wait a moment!'

He darted swiftly up the hall, and peered down the stairs to the basement. Then, as quickly, he darted back again.

''Ere—don't keep bobbin' abart like that!' complained the seaman weakly. 'It's narsty.'

'I wanted to be sure there *wasn't* anything below,' explained Fordyce.

'Well, that's silly,' retorted the seaman, ''cos yer can't be sure o' hennythink in this 'ouse . . . Oi! Wotcher lookin' at?'

Fordyce's eyes were now fastened on the door, through which the fog was pouring.

'Better close it, I think,' he murmured.

'Fust bit o' sense you've spoke,' agreed the seaman. 'But I wouldn't bolt it, guv'nor.'

'Why not?'

'We might wanter git hout agin quick.'

'You mean you might,' responded Fordyce, as he closed the door. 'Well, come along. Let's be getting up.'

He turned towards the staircase. Carpetless and grubby, with its balustrade broken and incomplete, it made an appropriate beginning to an ascent which was to terminate in a corpse. Fordyce eyed it speculatively, while his odd companion observed:

'Pretty bit o' arkiteckcher, ain't it? But it ain't a patch on wot yer'll find 'igher hup.'

'Yes, you know these stairs pretty well, don't you?' replied Fordyce.

'Wotcher mean?'

'Well—you've been up and down them pretty often!'

'Yus. Like a bloomin' 'ousemaid.'

'Didn't you have a light or something?' queried Fordyce.

'Candle, guv'nor.'

'Well, where is it? A little illumination would certainly be cheerful.'

'Blimy if I knows where it is, I come dahn in sich a 'urry. I 'ad it then—yus, 'corse I did. I must 'ave dropped it—'

'And there it is, old son, by your foot. Pick it up, will you?'

'No, thanks,' grunted the seaman, shaking his head.

'You are a goose! Why not? It won't bite you!'

'Nah, but if I bends dahn, p'r'aps yer'll sit on me 'ead agin like yer did larst time.'

Fordyce smiled, picked up the candle, and lit it.

''Ere come the shadders,' murmured the seaman.

'And here come us,' answered Fordyce, giving his companion a shove. 'By the way, what's your name?'

'Ben. Ben, o' the Merchant Service. Nosey, ain't yer?'

'Ben what?'

'It'd be Ben Bolt, if it wasn't fer you, guv'nor!'

'Ha! Well, I don't mind your bolting, so long as you bolt in the right direction. Bolt up those stairs. Yes—you first.' He gave him another shove. 'For goodness' sake, do get a move on!'

'Well, I'm a-goin', ain't I?' grumbled Ben, as he began to climb. 'Think I'm a bloomin' Zeppelin?'

Conversation lapsed for a few seconds. Fordyce was keeping his eyes and ears well open, while Ben's gloomy thoughts, as they drew nearer and nearer their grim objective, weighed upon him. But when they were half-way up the first flight, the seaman stopped suddenly.

'What's wrong?' demanded Fordyce.

'I s'pose yer knows, guv'nor,' said Ben, 'that there's somethink waitin' fer us up at the top?'

'Yes. A corpse.'

'More'n that, I reckons. Wot abart the bloke wot done 'im in? And them noises?'

'You've got noises on the brain. Gee up!' exclaimed Fordyce.

'I tells yer, there's *things* hup there,' insisted Ben. 'Things! 'Ouse is 'aunted. And there's things *dahnstairs*.'

'Yes, and there are things *on* the stairs!'

'Gawd!' gasped the seaman. 'Where?'

'Here. *Us*. You and me. Get along!'

''Ere, stow that,' muttered Ben. 'You orter've bin hon these stairs, like I was once, in the middle o' the night. Shufflin' noises above me. Rushin' steps below me. Inter the Valley o' Death, and no mistike!'

'What did you do?'

'Wot's the meat do in a sandwidge? Stay where it is! So I stays on these stairs a hour, afeared to go hup, and afeared to go dahn.'

'Well, for the Lord's sake, go up now!'

'Orl right, orl right!' He continued his grudging climb, but almost the next moment he had stopped again. 'Oh, Gawd!' he murmured.

'I wish you'd vary your language a bit,' complained Fordyce. 'What's happened now?'

'Bumped me 'ead.'

'Well, of course you'll bump your head if you keep on stopping!'

'Garn! I only keeps on stoppin' 'cos I bumps me 'ead . . . Nah, then! 'Oo's a-stoppin' *nah*?'

'Wait a moment,' whispered Fordyce, and held his candle up to the wall. 'What's this?'

'Wot's wot?' asked Ben fearfully.

Fordyce peered hard at a mark, and the seaman peered with him, his mouth hung open in an agony of suspense.

'My mistake,' said Fordyce, giving him a prod. 'I thought it was *ber-lud*!'

''Ere, guv'nor!' moaned Ben. 'Stow that! Me legs won't stand it!'

'Well, frankly, I don't wonder your nerves are a bit shaky

after a night in this god-forsaken place,' conceded Fordyce, as Ben began to move on again.

'Shaky? That's right,' nodded the seaman. 'But they ain't no more shaky than these 'ere stairs. Mind that step, guv'nor.'

'Which one?'

'This one. It ain't there.'

'And maybe our corpse won't be there, either. You know, my friend, this is a grand spot for imagination. Why, once I even imagined you were moving.'

'I can move when I likes to, don*choo* worry! But I got roomertism in me 'ip. Wot abart you goin' a'ead?'

'No, thanks.'

'Why not?'

'You know as well as I do. If you were behind, you'd *stay* behind.'

''Ow well yer knows me, guv'nor,' said Ben sarcastically.

'Yes, I feel as though we're quite old pals by now.'

They reached the top of the first flight. Fordyce looked about him before ascending the next. The ground beneath them began to vibrate.

'Hallo! What's that?' he exclaimed.

'That ain't nothin,' guv'nor,' replied Ben. 'That's only a trine. Tunnel goes hunder this 'ouse.'

'All the advantages,' murmured Fordyce.

'Tunnel to 'Arwich, I reckons. Yer'll 'ar plenty of that.'

The train grew louder, and rumbled below them . . .

'Hallo—*that* wasn't a train!' whispered Fordyce, the next moment.

'Lummy!' gasped Ben.

A door had banged somewhere in the house, but whether above them or below them they could not say. The rumbling of the train had half-deadened the sound, and confused the acoustics. In his terror, Ben backed against Fordyce, and the candle went out.

'Oi!' shouted Ben, now beside himself. 'Oi!'

'What's the matter!' Fordyce shouted back angrily.

'Light's gorn hout!'

'Well, I know that! You are the biggest dolt! You bumped into me, and made me drop it—but it's easy enough to light it again, isn't it? Oh, for goodness' sake, man, do pull yourself together!'

Stooping, Fordyce regained the candle, and struck a match. It flared on two oddly contrasted faces: Fordyce's, grim, anxious, but determined; Ben's livid with stark fear. All the way up, the sailor had done his best to keep steady, and his occasional flashes of humour had reflected his spasmodic attempts to get above himself. But now they were actually on the verge of seeing the corpse again. Would it be lying still and silent as he had left it? Or would the being or creature that had attacked it be in its place, waiting for some fresh victim?

The banging door and the sudden darkness had reduced Ben to zero again. Every time he tried to set his spirit up, something came along to knock it down again!

'Guv'nor,' he said hoarsely, as his ruthless companion applied the match to the candle-wick. 'Look 'ere. I sye. Let's quit!'

'Rot!' answered Fordyce. 'It's not my habit to quit.'

'Yus—but wot abart *my* 'abit?'

'Rot again! It shouldn't be your habit. And, besides, I'm enjoying this!' He held up the candle. 'There we are. The sun's shining again. And here's the last lap. Come along!'

''Ow many more times are yer goin' ter say, "Come hon!"' mumbled Ben.

'Just as many times as you *don't* "come hon,"' answered Fordyce. 'Judging by past experience, that means about ten million times.'

They ascended the last flight. As Ben had said, it was infinitely worse than the lower flight. Twice the seaman stumbled, but possibly that was not entirely the fault of the stairs.

When they reached the small top landing, Ben stopped dead, but Fordyce pushed him ruthlessly forward through the wide-open door.

'Now, then—where is it?' demanded Fordyce.

'There, guv'nor!' whispered Ben, and pointed a trembling finger towards the inner room.

9

The Corpse

The door leading to the inner room was wide open and in the aperture, half in shadow and half revealed by the flickering firelight, lay a huddled form. Grim enough at the best of times, the room looked doubly grim now with the sullen, shooting shadows, the little arc of light made by the candle, and that huddled, silent figure.

The very walls, with their peeling paper, were sinister. The room was charged with the gloom of a recent tragedy—a tragedy so recent that its emotions hung heavy on the air, and the auras of those concerned in it lingered yet around the still form in the aperture. Ben's eyes were almost comic in their fear, while even Gilbert Fordyce could not repress a little shudder.

'By Jove,' he murmured. 'You were right! The real thing, eh?'

''Corse it's the real thing,' muttered Ben. 'Didn't I tell yer?'

Fordyce's glance swept swiftly over the room. Then he

crossed quickly to the body and bent over it. It was the form of a man with a crooked shoulder.

'Dead, ain't 'e, guv'nor?' whispered Ben, across the room. He had not followed his leader to the prone figure, but had backed towards a pile of wooden cases.

Fordyce did not reply at once. He was beginning to feel the body. But he jumped up with a start as a sudden crash fell upon his ears. Ben stood, jibbering, beside a fallen case.

'What on earth are you doing?' barked Fordyce testily.

'Sorry, guv'nor,' chattered Ben. 'Jest wobbled a bit, like.'

'Well, don't wobble a bit like any more! How do you suppose I can get on with this if you don't pull yourself together a bit?'

He turned back to the corpse, and began to examine it again.

'Wot's done it, guv'nor?' asked Ben.

'Seems to have been hit on the head—coming out of that room.'

'Yus, but 'oo 'it 'im?' asked Ben hoarsely. 'That's wot beats me. 'Oo 'it 'im?'

'We'll have to try to find out. Perhaps—'

He paused, and glanced towards the inner chamber. Though the door was wide, only a portion of it was revealed, and even that portion was in shadow. Ben followed his gaze, and gulped convulsively.

'P'r'aps—wot?' he quavered.

'He may be in there—eh?' said Fordyce, in a low voice.

He had put the candle on the floor. Now taking it up suddenly, he slipped quickly into the adjoining room.

'Oi! Oi!' bellowed Ben.

'What's the matter?' shouted Fordyce, returning immediately.

Ben looked at him, a trifle shamefacedly.

'Yer—yer left me in the dark, guv'nor,' he said.

'Idiot!'

'G'arn! Idjit yerself. Yer seems ter fergit that there candle's mine!'

'Well, I've borrowed it—as I've no doubt you did yourself. Tell me—is there an exit through that room there?'

'Hexit?'

'Yes! Don't keep repeating what I say, and staring like a fish! Is there an exit—a way out, or anything?'

'No, guv'nor,' replied Ben. 'It's jest a room—like this 'un. There ain't no hother door, nor nothin'.'

Fordyce disappeared again, stepping carefully over the form on the floor, and once more Ben was left in darkness. He slithered round to the fireplace, but as he drew near it suddenly crackled, and he sprang back.

'Gawd!' he muttered miserably. 'Even the blinkin' fire's a-spittin' at me nah!'

He sprang back so far that he found himself near the passage door.

'Well, why not?' he thought. 'I've showed 'im the bloomin' plice. Nah 'e can 'ave it! 'E ain't got no right ter keep me 'ere!'

He turned, and began to tiptoe away. A hand descended on his shoulder, and a grave voice behind him observed:

'You know, if you're not very careful, you'll put a rope round your neck.'

The wretched man wheeled round, and once more faced his tormentor.

'Wotcher mean?' he gasped. 'I was on'y jest—wotcher mean?'

Fordyce looked at him steadily.

'I mean,' he said, 'it never hurts an innocent man to play straight.'

''Oo ses I'm a hinnercent man?' retorted Ben. That didn't sound quite right; he corrected himself. 'I mean, 'oo ses I ain't a-playin' stright?'

'Are you *quite* sure you've had no hand in this, my man?'

'S'elp me 'Eving, I 'aven't,' answered Ben piously.

'Have another think?' suggested Fordyce.

Indignation stirred in Ben's breast.

''Ave another think?' he retorted. 'Wot's the good o' thinkin'? If I'd 'a done it, I'd 'a knowed it, wouldn't? D'yer s'pose one fergits a murder like postin' a letter? Look 'ere—'

'Steady, steady,' interposed Fordyce soothingly. 'Don't get so excited. I'm inclined to believe you—that's honest. But we've got to clear this mystery up, and it's no good getting touchy.'

'Oh, no hoffence, *I'm* sure!' observed Ben, to the ceiling. ''Oo'd mind a little thing like being took fer a murderer? Fancy being 'urt!' Fordyce smiled, despite himself, and Ben jumped in eagerly on the softening tide. 'Look 'ere, guv'nor,' he said, 'you torks abart clearin' this hup, but wot's it our business, any'ow? 'Tain't your business, see? 'Tain't my business, see? It's the perlice's business, see? As I ses orl along. It's the perlice's business. Git a bobby.'

The plea was eloquent, but ineffective. To Ben's disappointment, Fordyce shook his head. Ben had never met such an annoying, persistent fellow in all his born days.

'Sorry, but I think we'll still postpone that bobby for a bit, if you don't mind,' said Fordyce. 'Of course, we'll have to bring him along presently, though. You say you've been alone in this house?'

'Gawd, 'e's orf agin!' thought Ben, as he nodded his head.

'All alone!'

'Yus.'

'Who made that fire?'

'I did,' answered Ben defiantly. 'Didn't want ter freeze, did I?' Noting Fordyce's roving eye upon the empty food tin, he anticipated the next question. '*Hor* ter starve. You're a Nosey Parker, ain't yer? Pork an' beans, guv'nor. Puzzle, find the pork. *That* wasn't no meal fer two. Lorblimy, it wasn't no meal fer *one*—but it's the last I've 'ad. I tell yer, I've got a 'ole in me inside the size of a—'

Fordyce waved him down. He was sorry for the poor man's hunger, but reiteration interfered with one's train of thought.

'Suppose someone was in the house without your knowing it?' he suggested.

'Then 'e was pretty nippy at 'idin' 'isself,' answered Ben. 'But, o' corse, there was them noises I told yer abart.'

A train rumbled beneath them.

'That kind of a noise?' queried Fordyce.

'No! Not that! That's a trine—tunnel ter 'Arwich, wot I sed. There was them footsteps—creepin', creepin'—'

'Yes, yes, yes. I have gathered already that they crept. But one mistakes noises sometimes, you know. Particularly in the middle of the night. Do you think they might have been creaks?'

'Yus, they might. But did yer ever 'ear of a creak wot 'it a man on the 'ead?'

He jerked his thumb towards the body, and Fordyce smiled.

'Now, listen, old son,' said Fordyce. 'If you didn't hit him on the head—'

'Say that agin', guv'nor, and I'll 'it you on the 'ead, so I will!' grunted Ben.

'Shut up! If you didn't, somebody else must have, and that somebody else must have been in this house when you first entered it—'

'There wasn't no one, guv'nor, that I'll lay to!'

'Then he must have slipped into the house without your noticing it.'

''Ow could 'e? There's only two doors, guv'nor. Back an' front. I kep' 'em both bolted.'

'Yes—in the night, yes. But you told me you'd left the front door ajar just now, didn't you?'

'Yus. That's right . . . Lummy!'

'You know,' said Fordyce reprovingly, 'you're going the wrong way to work. If you want to clear yourself of suspicion, you ought to try and prove that someone else *has* been in the house. Isn't that clear to you?'

Ben considered the point.

'Well,' he said, 'we knows somebody helse 'as bin in the 'ouse.'

'Do we? Who?'

''Im.'

Ben jerked his thumb towards the corpse.

'You are a charming dolt,' sighed Fordyce. 'Somebody *besides* him. Well, I see you can't help me. Let's have a look at your pockets.'

Ben backed away. This, surely, was becoming unnecessarily personal.

'Wotcher mean?' he exclaimed indignantly. 'Ain't even me pockets me own?'

'Come along,' insisted Fordyce. 'Turn 'em out.'

''Oo'd be a little man?' grumbled Ben. 'Yer wouldn't hask ter see me pockets, not if I was Dempsey.'

'Maybe not, old chap. But you're not Dempsey, so we

won't worry about it. Turn 'em out. What have you got in them?'

''Oles,' replied Ben. Fordyce took a step towards him. 'Orl right, orl right. 'Ave it yer own way. But I can't mike yer hout, guv'nor, so I carn't! One minit, I *'as* done it. Next minit, blimy, I *'asn't* done it. It's heasy ter see you ain't no perfeshunal 'tec!'

'Trouser pockets first,' commanded Fordyce.

Ben produced a dirty red rag. 'Ankerchiff,' he observed. 'Used that ter gag 'im . . . Bit o' string. Strangled 'im with that . . . Pencil. Real lead. That's wot I 'it 'im on the 'ead with. That's orl.'

'No, not quite,' responded Fordyce. 'There's something else you began to take out of your left-hand pocket, and then you slipped it back again.'

'Never mind abart that,' said Ben. ''Ave yer got to see the 'ole shop?'

'Let's have a look at it.'

'I said never mind abart that!'

'Got to use force?'

'Oh, 'ell!' muttered Ben. 'Blimy, if yer couldn't borrer a fiver orf the King! 'Ere it is!'

He dived his hand back into his left-hand pocket, and produced a little photograph. It was very shabby, but the grubbiness really didn't matter. It was a picture of a pretty little girl.

'I beg your pardon,' murmured Fordyce sympathetically, as he took the picture, and studied it. 'Yours?'

'Yus,' nodded Ben.

'Jolly little kid,' smiled Fordyce, handing the little piece of pasteboard back.

'Yus,' muttered Ben. 'She—was.' A sudden silence fell

upon the room. Ben felt it necessary to break it. 'Oh, 'ere's somethink helse,' he said, fishing out a bit of a cigarette. ''Arf a fag. One o' Lord Rothschild's. 'E smokes one hend, see, and I smokes the hother.'

'Then I don't think I'll volunteer for the middle,' remarked Fordyce.

'Oi, wot abart *your* pockets?' suggested Ben. 'Fair's fair!'

'I don't think we'll trouble about mine,' replied Fordyce.

'Oh, orl right,' sniffed Ben. 'I'll let yer orf—I ain't sich a Nosey Parker as you—'

'Got an idea about these noises,' interposed Fordyce suddenly. 'Could they have been rats?'

For the first time, Ben laughed.

'Not unless they was rats on roller-skates,' he said. 'More likely, guv'nor, they was *ghosts*!'

'H'm,' grunted Fordyce. 'I'll believe in ghosts when I see one. What about vibration?'

'Vi 'oo?'

'Vibration—the shaking of the trains, you know.'

'Yer orf yer nut, guv'nor! Vibrashun!'

'Well, we've got to think of everything—possible and impossible—and I thought—man alive, what's the matter *now*?'

'Lor' luvvaduck!' chattered Ben, crumpling up again. 'Look there, guv'nor—that—door!'

'Eh? What door?' cried Fordyce, wheeling round.

Ben was staring at the door which he had been unable to open—the door on the wall opposite the fireplace. His eyes nearly popped out of his head, and Fordyce followed his gaze, expecting the door to open. But nothing happened, and, as far as he could see, the door called for no special comment.

'Oh, I see what you mean,' he exclaimed suddenly. 'We've not looked in that cupboard yet.'

He moved towards it, but an exclamation from Ben detained him.

''Arf a mo', 'arf a mo'!' jabbered Ben. 'I 'aven't—there wasn't—I—I couldn't hopen it, guv'nor—'

'Couldn't open it, man?' retorted Fordyce, thoroughly puzzled. 'Why, don't you know how to turn a key?'

'Yus,' gulped Ben.

'Then, in heaven's name, why *didn't* you turn it?' demanded Fordyce, frowning.

''Cos the larst time I was in this room, guv'nor,' whispered Ben hoarsely, '*there wasn't no key there!*'

10

In the Cupboard

Few things in the inanimate world are more potent to produce emotion than a door. The lover's heart bounds with joy as he watches it for the approach of his sweetheart. At another time, the same heart may jump with fear as the same bit of wood slowly opens to admit heaven knows what! And cupboard doors, despite the fact that they have been designed to contain good things, can become the most sinister of all, for whereas the door of a house or of a room may be a mere channel from one unsavoury event to another, the door of a cupboard suggests some definite incident or terminal point. 'Come in, and discover strange happenings,' is the message of the front door. The message of the cupboard door is, 'Here, it happened!'

Gilbert Fordyce had already opened one cupboard door in that house. This was the cupboard door in the adjoining room; and, although he had not confessed it to Ben, he had not found the operation precisely pleasurable. Happily the cupboard in the adjoining room had merely proved large and empty. But would this cupboard prove the same?

It was the key in the door that provided its chief uncanniness. Apparently, the key had only recently been inserted. During the period of Ben's last absence, in fact. Who had inserted that key—the figure now lying on the floor, or someone who had attacked the figure? And what lay inside the cupboard, to provide its special interest?

Another question rose on top of these, and by its disturbing nature eclipsed them. Had the purpose of the cupboard been accomplished—or was that purpose still in process of accomplishment?

Fordyce pulled himself together, and addressed the seaman in a lowered voice.

'Are you *sure* that key wasn't there before?' he asked quietly.

'Yus, guv'nor,' nodded Ben, committing the anomaly of shaking his head at the same time.

'How are you sure?'

''Ow? Wotcher mean?'

'It might have been there, and you mightn't have noticed it,' suggested Fordyce.

'It weren't there, guv'nor,' insisted Ben. 'Yer see, I tried ter git it hopen more'n once.'

'And it was locked?'

'Yus. And the key weren't there, I tells yer.'

Fordyce advanced a step, then paused, with his eyes on the bottom of the door.

'What about that bolt?' he inquired. 'Was that drawn? As it is now?'

The bolt was six inches above the floor, forming another grimly suggestive item. Cupboards do not usually have both keys and bolts on the outside.

'No—I done that,' muttered Ben. 'I done that when I

tries ter git it open. But it was locked, as I ses, and there weren't no—'

'All right, look here. I've got an idea.'

'Wot?'

'*You* open it!'

Ben backed away promptly, and nearly backed into the corpse. Then he backed back again, in the opposite direction, and came to roost against one of the wooden cases under the window.

'Gawd, wot a 'ouse!' he gasped. He stared at Fordyce with sudden indignation. 'Me hopen it? Wotcher tike me for?'

'Well, you know,' murmured Fordyce, 'it's your turn. I think I once heard you observe, "Fair's fair."'

'Garn!'

Fordyce shrugged his shoulders, and abruptly walked to the cupboard. 'Your heroism is a constant marvel to me,' he remarked. 'I don't know how you do it.' His conversation was something in the style of a dentist who is trying to soothe his patient while he takes out the forceps. He laid his fingers on the key and tested it. 'Well, it's locked now, anyway,' he reported.

Then Ben got an idea.

'Wot abart *leavin'* it locked?' he suggested.

'No, we can't do that,' replied Fordyce, and turned the key. 'Now—it's not locked.'

'Oi! Steady, there!' breathed Ben.

Fordyce paid no attention to him, but suddenly swung the door open. Immediately afterwards, he gave an exclamation.

Ben put his hands up, but as no one had jumped out of the cupboard, and there was no scuffle, he ventured the next moment to draw closer, and peer into the cupboard as Fordyce was doing.

It was certainly an odd cupboard. It ran some way into the wall, its end being in shadow, yet sufficiently discernible to reveal a bend, and along the right wall was a narrow shelf. A bit of broken mirror lay on the shelf, a brush, and a comb, while above, on hooks, hung a couple of wigs.

'Well, I'm dashed,' murmured Fordyce, as Ben peered over his shoulder. 'Look at that! Seems to be a sort of actor's dressing-room, eh?'

Ben did not reply. He was peering beyond the shelf and the wigs, at the shadowed end of the cupboard, with its concealed angle.

'Extraordinarily stout door, too, isn't it?' went on Fordyce. 'Mighty thick, for a cupboard. And padded. That's funny. Hallo—what's this?'

Upon the inside of the cupboard door was pinned a newspaper cutting. It was headed, in large type:

'THE GET-AWAY GUILD.'
HOW PRISONERS ESCAPE.
IS THERE A SECRET WAY TO THE CONTINENT?

Fordyce read this out, and also the beginning of the. paragraph which started beneath:

'"For some time the police have been trying to tap the activities of a secret organisation which is believed to be in existence for the purpose of helping 'wanted' people out of the country."'

'P'r'aps they could do me a bit o' good,' murmured Ben.

'Shut up! "A similar society is known to exist in Budapest—"'

'Oi,' interposed Ben, again. 'Ain't that enuff? 'Owjer know there ain't someone listenin' rahnd that corner there? 'Ave a look!'

Fordyce smiled. 'Anything to please you,' he observed, and entered the cupboard.

Ben watched him anxiously. He watched him disappear completely round the bend, at the end. His anxiety grew, as he watched and waited for the reappearance.

'Oi!' he called hoarsely. 'Are you still there?' Then he jumped back, as Fordyce reappeared. 'Yer know, guv'nor,' he murmured faintly, 'I'll go barmy if I 'as much more o' this—stright, I will!'

'Well, I'm not sure that I'd blame you,' frowned Fordyce. 'This is, without exception, the queerest house I've ever been in!'

'Wot did yer find in there?'

'Nothing. Only cobwebs. I—Sh!' He darted to the passage door, and listened.

'Oh, lummy!'

'Sh! Quiet! Yes—keep your nerve now!' muttered Fordyce. 'There's someone coming upstairs!'

'Then go hout and 'it 'im!' chattered Ben.

'Quiet!' hissed Fordyce.

All at once he jumped aside, silently, like a cat. Standing now by the door, and still listening intently, he clenched his fists. Ben's fists were also clenched—over his stubby chin.

Creak—creak—creak. The steps had now reached the top of the stairs, and the thing that had caused them was pausing on the landing. In another second, it would come on again, the door would open . . .

'Oi!' shouted Ben, at the top of his voice.

'Fool!' barked Fordyce, and flung the door wide.

But, as he did so, there was a scuttle, and the thing descended again like lightning. A black shadow, and it was gone. Before Fordyce could hurl himself after it, he felt two arms gripped round his leg.

'What the—!' he cried, swinging round again.

Ben was on his knees, holding him.

'Let go!' shouted Fordyce angrily.

The grip loosened, and Ben stared up at him like a lunatic.

'Sived yer life that time, guv'nor, I did,' he gurgled. 'It—it 'd 'ave 'ad yer!'

'Oh, you fool, you fool!' groaned Fordyce, and, freed now, ran out of the room.

But, on the landing, he again paused.

'I say!' he called back. 'This skylight's open! Did you know it?'

'Wot's that?'

'By Jove, we ought to have noticed that. We—we've not examined the roof yet.'

Instead of running downstairs, Fordyce returned to the room. Gripping the wobbling specimen of the Merchant Service by the shoulders, he spoke quickly and decisively.

'Now, listen—if you can!' he said. 'I'm going down after that fellow. Is it any use taking you with me?'

'Not a bit o' use,' replied Ben, with no less decision.

'I believe you're right.'

'I *knows* I'm right!'

'Very well, then. I'll leave you. But, for God's sake, see if you can't pull yourself together a bit while I'm gone.' Ben blinked at him, and he added in exasperation, 'Upon my soul, when we're through with this, I'll recommend you for the Victoria Cross. You're quite the pluckiest lad I've ever struck.'

'It's orl very well fer you, guv'nor,' mumbled Ben, as Fordyce turned away. 'You've got beef an' greens in yer stummick. 'Oo could be a 'ero on a hempty stummick?'

Fordyce did not hear him. He was out on the landing, and a clicking noise suddenly made Ben raise his eyes.

'Oi!' shouted Ben, and rushed to the door. It was closed, and he turned the knob fruitlessly. 'Darn 'is eyes! 'E's locked me hin!'

He turned round slowly. The firelight flickered faintly on the huddled figure in the aperture. He backed against the wall. Was it his imagination—or had the corpse moved?

11

Across the Roof

Whatever kind of a time Gilbert Fordyce was having below, Ben's own position was not more enviable. He was locked in a room with a gaping cupboard door on one side, and a corpse on the other.

The very stillness of the moment seemed to invite interruption from either the corpse or the cupboard. Both were points of evil, from which any terror might emerge. For a full minute Ben stood motionless. Then time, that towers so mightily above our emotions, worked its change, and Ben's frenzy began to pass.

'P'r'aps Charlie didn't move,' he thought. 'P'r'aps—it was jest me own 'ead wobblin', like.'

That might well have been. It wobbled now from the corpse to the cupboard, and focused itself upon the dim interior.

'Think I'll close it,' was his next thought. The frenzy past, he was growing constructive. 'Yus—I'll close it. An' lock it, too. Then nothin' narsty can't come poppin' hout!'

He slithered gingerly around the wall, and slowly closed

the cupboard door. The first part of the operation was slow, at least, but the last part was rapid, the sudden speed being impelled by the thought that, if he were not quick, some unseen inmate of the cupboard might try to push the door open against him. He closed the door, and bolted it. 'Ooray! *That* was done!

Next he turned to the fire. It was low; and, of course, Fordyce had taken the solitary candle.

'Seems ter think the 'ole bloomin' plice belongs to 'im,' grumbled Ben. 'Let's git a bit of a blize.'

He collected some wood, and crossing the room carefully, keeping one eye cocked on the corpse as he drew nearer it, he threw the wood on the fire. For a few seconds it extinguished what light there was, but soon it began to spit and spurt and crackle, and a great blaze shot up.

'There, that's a bit more like it!' thought Ben. 'Me mother sed I wasn't ter be lef' in the dark!'

Warmed by the additional illumination, he became bold enough to approach even closer to the corpse, and to pay definite attention to it.

''Allo, Charlie,' he said. ''Ow are yer?'

The corpse did not reply, happily for Ben's sanity. The firelight glinted on its upturned boots. It glinted, also, on a hand, a shoulder, and the upper part of the face. Ben found his eyes resting on the hunched shoulder.

'Proper crooked, ain't it?' he thought. 'Crooked like 'isself, I'll lay!'

Then the firelight glinted on something else, and all at once Ben crept forward, and drew that something from the prone man's pocket.

'Blimy!' he gasped. '*Bricelets!*'

He rose, and held the handcuffs up. That was a bit of

a puzzle, that was! What was the man doing with *handcuffs* in his pocket?

This discovery, coupled with the assurance that the corpse did not bite, increased Ben's courage further, and he approached the corpse again, to see whether he could find anything else. He did not like the work. The man had a nasty wound in his head, and in order to reach another pocket with a likely bulge to it, the body had to be rolled over on its side. The operation was worth it, however, for the second bulge proved to be a revolver. Ben's eyes popped when he grasped this useful weapon.

'Well, I'm blowed,' he muttered. 'A gun! 'Ere's a bit o' luck!' He glanced towards the passage door. 'Nah I can stop any fancy tricks. Bit of orl right, this is!'

He slipped the revolver into his own pocket, and then, staring down at the unpalatable sight, decided to remove it. Already it was two parts in the inner room. Stooping quickly, Ben gave it a shove and a roll, and managed to get it through the aperture. Then he closed the door to the adjoining room, and locked it.

'Good-bye, Charlie!' he said. 'We carn't 'ave yer in the best parler. Sorry, but I don't like the look o' yer!'

With the revolver in his pocket, Ben felt considerably better, and the room began to wear a less forbidding aspect. All the same, there was no harm in exploring all its possible exits, and he climbed on to the wooden cases under the window. As he did so, a clock in the distance faintly chimed the quarter after four.

He soon climbed down again. Despite the thick fog, he had seen enough to convince him that it was a pretty big drop, and that there was no escape for him that way.

He had taken out his revolver, and was re-examining it,

when he heard steps outside. Back went the revolver into his pocket, but he kept his hand there as the key turned, the door opened, and Fordyce reappeared, a frown of perplexity on his face.

'This beats me altogether!' exclaimed Fordyce. 'I went right down—' He paused abruptly. 'Hallo! What have you been up to?'

'Wotcher mean?' demanded Ben, falling back on his usual formula.

'What do I mean? Why, where's our corpse?'

'Oh, *'im*! I stowed 'im away in the nex' room, guv'nor.'

'Prize idiot!' said Fordyce. 'Don't you know it's not usual to remove corpses before the police have had a look at them?'

'Ain't it?' replied Ben.

Fordyce glanced at him sharply. He vaguely sensed something new in the seaman's attitude, but did not guess its cause. The next moment he gave another exclamation.

'Where—on—earth did *those* spring from?' he inquired, staring at the mantelpiece, where Ben had deposited the handcuffs.

'Fahnd 'em in 'is pocket, guv'nor,' responded Ben cheekily.

'That's rum!'

'Yus. Ain't it? Wot are they?'

'What, never seen a pair of handcuffs before?' asked Fordyce, smiling.

'Not me,' said Ben. 'Hor felt 'em.'

'Well, let's hope you never will,' commented Fordyce. 'While you made progress up here, I drew a blank downstairs. But there's the roof yet. I'm a bit curious about that.'

'Are yer?' retorted Ben, as Fordyce walked to the chair, and laid his hand upon it.

'Yes, I am,' answered Fordyce sharply.

'Well, yer can 'ave the roof, 'Arold Lloyd,' observed Ben. 'I'm goin'.'

Fordyce turned to Ben, and regarded him squarely. There was something in Fordyce's look Ben did not quite like, but he decided to make a stand, before his courage ebbed again.

'Yus, I'm goin',' he repeated. 'I ain't goin' hon with this, I ain't, and you ain't got no right ter keep me 'ere, you ain't. See? It's a free country. See? This is a bobby's job. Messin' abart. That's wot it is. Messin' abart!'

'Finished?' inquired Fordyce politely.

'Wotcher mean, "finished"?' sulked Ben.

If only Fordyce had lost his temper, Ben might have lost his. But Fordyce knew better than to lose his temper.

'I mean, I *hope* you've finished,' said Fordyce, 'because I hate to see you waste your breath. And you don't seem to realise one thing, my man—something I've realised all along.'

'Wot's that?'

'Why, that any delay in getting that bobby is all in your favour. I'm wasting all this time on your behalf as much as on anybody's. You see, if we don't find out something more before that policeman pays his little call, you'll probably find him taking out his notebook, and asking you some very awkward questions. Let that sink in a bit.'

'But—I ain't done it!' exclaimed Ben desperately. 'I ain't *done* it, I tells yer!'

'Well, I'm not saying you have,' returned Fordyce. 'But it's on the cards that the police may take a different view, my son. It's lucky for you I found no weapon on you—nothing more murderous than a lead pencil.'

'Eh?' jerked Ben, his hand in his pocket closing convulsively.

'That'll be in your favour, anyway,' concluded Fordyce, and, turning away, took the chair out into the passage, and placed it under the skylight.

'Guv'nor!' cried Ben.

'Ease down,' replied Fordyce.

'I ain't goin' ter hease dahn! Not till yer tells me wot ye'r' goin' ter tell the perlice.'

'I am going to tell them neither more nor less than the truth,' Fordyce informed him. 'By Jove, how this fog is pouring in!'

'The truth, eh?'

'Yes. *Do* keep quiet for a minute!'

He was on the chair now. Ben made a bolt for it. Fordyce promptly jumped down, and shoved him back into the room.

'My God, you *are* an idiot!' he said earnestly. 'Don't you realise that you've got to depend largely upon my evidence? Don't chuck away your chance in this silly fashion!'

'Charnce!' panted Ben. 'A bloomin' charnce a feller like me 'as when a copper gits 'old of 'im. Look 'ere, guv'nor—let's 'ave it stright. Yer thinks I ain't got no guts. Well—p'r'aps I 'as! Nah, then. D'yer say I've done this 'ere murder, or don't yer?'

Fordyce considered the question carefully. Then he replied:

'I really don't think you've got the courage to murder anybody, if you want to know. It takes rather a lot of pluck, when it comes to the point. But, for the moment, we're all under suspicion.'

The reply was not wholly unsatisfactory. If it was uncomplimentary, it contained some comfort. Ben decided to postpone his trump card.

'S'long as we're *horl* hunder suspicion,' he observed slowly, 'it don't matter so much. That means you along o' me, guv'nor?'

'Yes. If you like.'

'I do like. Misery loves company. Nah, git on yer bloomin' roof. I'll stay 'ere, an' pick up the pieces.'

'Good for the Merchant Service,' smiled Fordyce, and jumped on the chair again.

But he was back in the room like a flash, and he did not need to tell Ben why. A soft, dragging sound had started overhead.

'Oh, my Gawd—wot's 'appenin' nah?' yelped Ben.

'Sh!' whispered Fordyce. 'It's—someone crawling across the roof.'

They stood still. There was no mistaking the sound. Nor was there any mistaking the direction. The crawler was making for the skylight.

'D-did yer say the winder was hopen?' gasped Ben.

'Yes,' whispered Fordyce.

'Then, for Gawd's sake, go an' close it!'

Fordyce took no notice of him. Swiftly he blew out the candle, an action that so startled and terrified Ben that he lost his voice entirely. As a little shower of plaster came down from the roof, Fordyce ran to the fire, and lifted a wooden case before it to block out the light. The room was now almost pitch-dark.

But a faint light filtered through the skylight into the passage on which their eyes were trained, and this remained until it was blocked by the crawling body. Then the body began to slip through.

12

The Girl Next Door

Ben had heard many things since he had entered that house barely twenty-four hours before, but this was the first living creature he had seen—the first real evidence (apart from the corpse, who was dead) that he had not been victimised from the start by a series of hallucinations, or by his own fevered imagination. And even now, while he stared with glazed eyes into the dimness of the little landing, the living creature was no more distinct than a shadow. A sudden intensity in a streak of the dimness suggested a leg, but there was not enough light to give the creature any definite shape, and in Ben's mind it might have been an ogre or some hairy monster.

In fact, so firmly fixed were his nameless, formless convictions concerning the intruder that his brain gave way, and he acted in blind obedience to terror. He stood the suspense as long as he could. He stood the descent of the creature from the skylight to the chair, and from the chair to the ground, and then its silent, groping forward towards the spot where they stood; but he could not wait till the creature touched him. With the shout of a frenzied beast, he hurled himself upon the creature, and grappled it to his terrified bosom.

The creature shrieked, and seemed to melt in his arms. Its slight weight, however, and his own momentum, brought them both to the ground. Then Ben heard someone swearing above him, he was rolled aside, and his brief tussle with the dragon was over.

'Gawd! Gawd!' he dithered.

'Strike a light, man! Quick!' rapped out Fordyce's voice in the darkness.

Ben did not move. Why should he move? There he was. Let the world roll on!

'A light, man, a light!' repeated Fordyce's voice angrily. 'Where are you? Are you hurt?'

'No,' Ben managed to mutter.

'Well, then, for heaven's sake, stop saying "Gawd" and light the candle—I can't move for a moment.'

Ben staggered to his feet. The responsibilities of this miserable life began to grip him again.

'The candle!' bawled Fordyce.

'I—I ain't got no matches,' chattered Ben.

'Well, I have! Here—my pocket. Can you feel? Quick! Right-hand side. I tell you, I can't move!'

Ben fumbled forward, and groped about the shape which, he concluded, must be Fordyce.

'No, no—*right*-hand pocket, I said!' rasped Fordyce.

'Well, 'ow do I know which way ye'r' facin'?' retorted Ben, and dived into the other pocket.

He found the matchbox, and tremblingly struck a match. As the light glowed, his eyes grew big.

'Blimy, guv'nor!' he muttered. 'It's a gal!'

'The *candle*, man!'

'Orl right, orl right.'

He dropped the match, lit another, and stumbled to the packing-case by the cupboard door on which the candle stood. Having lit the candle, he turned to look once more at the creature he had attacked. His relief was mingled with a certain indignation. What right had this slip of a girl to put blue fear into him?

She was a pretty girl. Pretty hair, she had. And he'd bet her eyes were pretty, too, when she opened them. Seemed sort of familiar, too, in a way. Hadn't he seen a girl like that once? It wasn't the girl at the inn—she hadn't been pretty like this one. Then who . . .

'Lummy, guv'nor!' cried Ben suddenly. 'I *knows* 'er!'

'What?' exclaimed Fordyce, who was holding her in his arms. 'You *know* her!'

'Yus. She lives nex' door.'

'What more do you know about her?' asked Fordyce.

'Nothin',' said Ben. 'I seed 'er yesterday, that's orl. Seed 'er on the doorstep, when 'er father goes hout. Finted, ain't she?'

'Yes. Thanks to you!'

'Well, 'ow was I ter know? 'Ow's hennybody ter know hennythink in this blinkin' 'ouse? Comin' hover the roof like that. Ain't that arskin' fer it?'

Fordyce looked at the closed eyes anxiously, and then glanced round the room.

'Run and get that chair in the passage, will you?' he said. 'I want to put her down, and give her a drop out of my flask.'

'Aye, aye,' replied Ben, and, walking carefully to the landing, came back with the chair without accident.

'Nice-lookin' gal, ain't she, guv'nor?' he commented, as Fordyce placed her on the chair.

'Now feel in my pocket again—other one, this time—and bring out the flask. I don't want to let go of her for a moment.'

'That's orl right, sir,' answered Ben. 'I knows 'ow ter give the dose. Reg'ler corpse reviver, ain't it?' But before he had prepared the dose, he called out, 'Oi! She's movin'!'

'Well, I can see that,' exclaimed Fordyce, as the girl gave a little shudder. 'Now, then. The flask—hand it to me.'

A few seconds later, the girl slowly opened her eyes, and stared dazedly around. A look of utter bewilderment spread over her features.

'Where—where am I?' she murmured.

Fordyce patted her shoulder quickly and reassuredly.

'Don't be afraid,' he said, in a quiet voice. 'You're among friends.'

She passed her hand across her forehead, and suddenly sat upright.

'Friends?' she faltered.

'Yes, friends,' repeated Fordyce. 'You're perfectly safe.'

'Where is he?' she cried abruptly.

'Where is—who?' inquired Fordyce.

The girl sank back again. 'I'm all confused!' she moaned. 'Please tell me who you are.'

'Certainly. My name's Gilbert Fordyce. And that's—Ben. I'm afraid I don't know his other name.'

'Merchant Service, miss,' said Ben. 'That'll find me.'

'I don't understand,' answered the girl, shaking her head wearily. 'Why are you here?'

'Well,' explained Fordyce, 'I happened to be passing the house when this fellow—' He paused. 'I say, Miss—?'

'Ackroyd. Rose Ackroyd.'

'Thank you. Well, Miss Ackroyd, suppose you tell us

why *you're* here, and then we'll tell you why *we* are. We're all trying to pierce the clouds, you know.'

'I'm—looking for my father,' replied the girl.

'Man with a crooked shoulder?' exclaimed Ben.

She faced him quickly.

'Why, what do you know of a man with a crooked shoulder?' she demanded.

Fordyce interposed. 'Oh, shut up, Ben!' he said testily. 'Let us hear what the lady has to say first.' Turning to Miss Ackroyd again, he asked, 'You say you're looking for your father, but what's happened to him?'

'I don't know,' she responded. 'But—I'm awfully frightened. I live next door, at No. 15. Dad and I live there alone.'

'Yus, I knows that, miss,' nodded Ben. 'Knows yer lives there, I mean. Saw yer yesterday, didn't I?'

'No, I don't remember—' she began, and then recognition came into her eyes. 'Oh, yes, I do remember now. You were in the street, weren't you, when my father went out?'

Fordyce looked at Ben quickly.

'Oh, you've seen Mr Ackroyd?' he exclaimed significantly.

'Well, I wouldn't say I've seed 'im, exackly,' corrected Ben. 'Jest a shadder in the fog, like.'

'You wouldn't—know him again, then?' queried Fordyce.

'Nah,' answered Ben, and winked towards the inner room behind Miss Ackroyd's back. 'That ain't—'

'Yes, yes, all right,' interrupted Fordyce, and turned back to the girl. 'You say you and your father live next door alone.'

'Yes.'

'All alone?'

'Yes—except when we have lodgers. We let rooms sometimes.'

'I see. And have you any lodgers now?'

She shook her head. 'No, we haven't had any for six months,' she said slowly. 'Not since—'

'Not since—when?' Fordyce encouraged her.

She shot a glance at Ben as she replied, 'Not since—since the man with the crooked shoulder left us.'

'Ah, that's 'im,' nodded Ben.

'Oh!' she cried, clasping her hands. 'What do you mean?'

'Oh, do shut up, there's a good chap!' burst out Fordyce, rounding on Ben angrily. 'Let me handle this!' To Rose Ackroyd he said, 'You tell me that this—man with the crooked shoulder left you six months ago?'

'Yes.'

'Have you seen him since?'

'No. He left rather suddenly, and, after that, Dad said he wasn't going to take any more lodgers. I don't know why. We've had plenty of chances, you know.'

'Well, I dare say your father has his reasons,' responded Fordyce. 'The room's empty n[illegible] Not used, eh?'

'Yes, it is used,' she answered, and shuddered slightly. 'Dad moved up into it.' She paused, as though afraid to say more.

'I suppose you know why your lodger left?' asked Fordyce.

'No, I don't know. He was often away for several days. He was away quite a long while sometimes. And presently he never came back at all. We never discovered the reason. At least—'

'Please go on, Miss Ackroyd,' urged Fordyce, as the girl hesitated.

'Well, I was going to say—*I* could never discover the reason. If Dad knew, he wouldn't tell me.'

She spoke reluctantly. She seemed anxious to tell her story, but something continually held her back.

'Wot was 'is nime, miss?' inquired Ben. 'This feller with a crooked shoulder?'

'Smith,' she said. 'At least, that was what he called himself. But I always had a funny feeling about him—I don't think that was his real name, somehow.' She shivered, and suddenly burst out, 'Oh, I'm sure you're friends, but why are you asking me all these questions?'

'Because, Miss Ackroyd,' answered Fordyce gravely, 'we're also trying to solve a mystery, and your mystery and ours seem bound up together. Please go on with your story . . . Oh, but just one moment! Have you been in this house before?'

'No, never,' she replied.

'I mean—this afternoon, you know?'

She shook her head.

'Quite sure o' that, miss?' queried Ben, staring at her fixedly.

'No! Why do you ask?' she exclaimed.

'Becos', miss, someun's bin 'ere—we've '*eard* things! And then—'

'I say, old son,' remarked Fordyce seriously, 'do you want me to shut you up in a cupboard?'

'Oh, 'ave it yer own way,' snorted Ben huffily. 'But why should you do orl the chin-waggin'?'

'Oh, dear—I'm so frightened,' murmured Rose. 'Please don't quarrel!'

'No fear of that—Ben and I understand each other,' Fordyce assured her cheerily. 'Now, then, let's hear your tale—and we'll both try not to interrupt. And, look here, Ben,' he added, 'while she's telling it, suppose you cut that candle in two? That will double the illumination.'

'Yus, I knows orl abart that, guv'nor,' retorted Ben, as he shuffled towards the candle. 'Yer wants ter keep me quiet!'

13

The Telegram

Then Rose Ackroyd told her story and a strange story it proved to be, as indeed it must have been to have culminated in a journey across a roof on a thick, foggy evening. It was so strange that, despite Gilbert Fordyce's promise, interruptions were frequent.

Yet perhaps the story was no stranger than the setting in which it was narrated: a bare room, illuminated by a wood fire and the shortened stump of a candle, the other portion of the candle-stump being prepared for separate ignition by an odd, half-defiant, half-terrorised seaman; the room occupied by three people who were strangers to each other, as they were strangers until recently to the room itself; with thick, impenetrable fog outside, the faint rumble, now and again, of trains running far beneath, a dead man behind one door, a mysterious cupboard behind another, and at least one invisible creature, creeping about the house. In such an environment as this, no ordinary tale would have fitted!

In a faltering voice, Rose began:

'My father's disappeared. He disappeared this afternoon. Only a little while ago—'

'Oh, then 'e come back arter I seed 'im go hout larst night?' interposed Ben.

'Yes. He wasn't away long then,' she answered. 'It was only some appointment—'

''Oo with?' Ben caught Fordyce's eye. 'Orl right. Sorry. Go hon.'

'I don't know who with,' the girl said. 'I didn't ask him, and he didn't tell me. Anyhow, he came back then, and nothing happened till after lunch today. Then he went up to his bedroom—'

Fordyce now committed the sin of interruption.

'Do you mean the room which your old lodger, Smith, used to have?' he asked.

'Yes. He goes there quite often, and spends a lot of time in the room with his door locked. I think he's got some important work or something—but he's never told me what it is. All I know is that it brings in a little money. Otherwise, you see, we'd simply *have* to take in some more lodgers, to make ends meet. We're—we're not so very well off, you see,' she added, with a slight flush.

Fordyce nodded sympathetically.

'A little while after he went up to his room this afternoon,' Rose resumed, 'a telegram came for him, and of course I went up to him with it. As a rule, I don't disturb him. He's told me not to, you see. It—seems to be very important work he's got, and—well, I'll tell you—it's sometimes worried me, he's so close about it. It seems to get on his mind.'

She paused. Fordyce nodded, and patted her shoulder reassuringly.

'I understand,' he said. 'Of course it must have worried you. You've no idea at all what the work is?'

'None at all. When I went to his room with the telegram, I found the door locked, as I'd expected, but what frightened me was when I knocked and didn't get any reply. I knocked a lot, and quite loudly. I had to, you see, because of the telegram. And then once, while I was knocking, I thought I heard a faint sound in the room. Of course—I got frightened.'

'Who wouldn't have?' exclaimed Fordyce. 'What did you do then?'

'I didn't know what to do. I said to myself, "Perhaps he's left the room, locked it after him, and gone out." But I know I must have heard him go. So then I began searching about the house for a key that would open the door.'

'Good idea! And you found one?'

'Yes, after a long while.' She suddenly covered her face with her hands. 'The room was empty!'

''Orrible!' muttered Ben, and hastily lit the second half of the candle for the comfort of the extra illumination.

'It *was* horrible,' continued Rose. 'I thought of all sorts of things. You know how one does. And then I noticed that the window was open—and one doesn't keep windows open on a foggy day like this, does one? I ran to the window and looked out. It opens on to a wide ledge. And when I looked out, I found—look—this little badge.'

She took a small badge out of her pocket, and showed it to Fordyce.

'That's odd,' commented Fordyce, and read: '"No. 17."'

'Sime number as this 'ouse, guv'nor,' said Ben, coming closer to have a look.

'So it is, Sherlock Holmes,' retorted Fordyce. '"No. 17—4.30."'

He looked at his watch suddenly, and Ben gave a little whoop.

'My Gawd—it's nearly that nah, ain't it, guv'nor?' he exclaimed.

'Not far off,' answered Fordyce seriously. 'Well, Miss Ackroyd—hallo—what's up, Ben?'

For Ben was staring at the badge with a new expression.

''Arf a mo', 'arf a mo'!' he cried. 'That's rum! I seed one o' them things afore!'

'What on earth do you mean?' demanded Fordyce, while Rose stared at him. 'Are you sure?'

'No, I ain't,' replied Ben. ''Cos, rightly speakin', I didn't see it at all, it was snatched aht o' me 'and too bloomin' quick. But she sed it 'ad "No. 17" hon it—'

'*Who* said?'

'The woman at the pub, guv'nor, where I was yesterday, on my way 'ere. Feller runs aht of a room. Hin I goes, picks this thing hup and then she snatches it aht o' me 'and. Then a bobby comes hin, and aht *I* goes. 'Corse I ain't sure abart it—'

'Well, if you're not sure, suppose we let Miss Ackroyd get on with her story?' suggested Fordyce, and turned to her again. 'Someone dropped the badge on the ledge, eh? And you suppose that someone was your father?'

'Yes,' she nodded.

'Well, what did you do then?'

'I crept out of the window—'

'Bit risky, wasn't it?'

'I didn't seem to think of that. But it's really quite easy

to get from the window to the roof. I *was* frightened, though, when I got on the roof. The fog was so thick. I crept across—'

'Lummy, miss, yer doesn't need ter tell us that,' interposed Ben. 'Yer give us the fair creeps!'

'Why? Did you hear me?'

'Did we 'ear yer?' murmured Ben, casting up his eyes. ''As kippers bones?'

'Well, well,' said Fordyce impatiently. 'You crept across the roof—?'

'Yes, and when I came to the other edge, I found it was an easy climb to the roof of No. 17—of this house, you know,' answered Rose. 'So I jumped from one roof to the other—'

'Damned plucky!' muttered Fordyce, under his breath.

'—and came to the skylight window. It was open. I slipped through—and then something sprang at me, and I fainted. And—that's all.'

'It was nothing worse than our friend Ben who sprang at you,' Fordyce informed her quickly. 'He means well, but he does odd things at times.'

'Garn—'oo wouldn't 'ave sprung at her?' retorted Ben. 'She never sounded 'er 'ooter!'

Rose shook her head wearily. 'There's something queer about this house—'

'Yus, it's 'aunted—'aunted proper!'

'Don't listen to him,' frowned Fordyce. 'What makes you say that?'

'Well, there's one thing I've noticed,' explained Rose. 'The queerest people come here. I've seen them sometimes, from the window. They don't look in the least like ordinary house-hunters—and if they *are* house-hunters, why doesn't one of them take the house? It's been to let for a very long while.'

'No one but a stark, starin' loonertick 'd tike this 'ouse, miss,' observed Ben.

'And then—oh, it all sounds very silly and foolish, I know—but letters keep on coming for Mr Smith, though he left months ago. Father always takes them. I don't know what he does with them. He *says* he directs them on, but only this morning I came upon an envelope addressed to Mr Smith that he'd—opened.' She broke in upon herself abruptly. 'Oh, why am I telling you all these things? You don't think I'm—disloyal, do you?'

'Not a bit. Of course not,' replied Fordyce kindly. 'I'm sure your father has some sound reason for his behaviour.'

'Thank you for saying that! I'm sure he has. He'd never do anything wrong—'

'By Jove, Miss Ackroyd—that telegram!' exclaimed Fordyce suddenly. 'What did you do with it?'

She stared at him, and then gave an exclamation of surprise.

'Why—I forgot all about it,' she answered, as she took the little orange envelope from her pocket. 'Here it is. I've not even opened it yet!'

'What about opening it now?' suggested Fordyce.

'Yes, yes—it may tell us something,' she cried, tearing it open quickly. In the act of taking out the form, she paused, 'You—you assure me, you *are* friends?'

'We'll prove it,' asserted Fordyce decisively.

She extracted the form, and, after a rapid survey of the message, read it aloud, wonderingly:

'"Keep clear No. 17 today. Sheldrake moving. Lie low till instructions. Suffolk necklace has been found. Barton."'

'Barton!' murmured Fordyce.

'That's the 'tec, ain't it?' queried Ben.

There was a silence. New thoughts and new activities were congregating in that room, yet they were no less confusing than the old.

'Does this telegram convey anything to you, Miss Ackroyd?' asked Fordyce.

'No, nothing,' she returned.

'Wot's yer father?' inquired Ben, following a brain-wave. 'In the jewellery business?'

'No. He's an insurance agent.'

There was another short silence, while each of them revolved the words of the telegram. Then Fordyce suddenly straightened himself, and exclaimed:

'Now, listen, Miss Ackroyd. The first thing you've got to do is to get it clear in your mind that I'm here to help you—'

'Oh, 'e's a great 'elp, 'e is,' interrupted Ben. ''E's done nothink but 'elp me fer the larst hour—when I comes rushin' hout o' this 'ouse shakin' like a haspen leaf, swipe me, 'e 'elps me rahnd and brings me back agin! Carn't do enuff fer yer, 'e carn't—!'

'Ease down, Ben, ease down!' barked Fordyce. 'You'd better get back to your house, Miss Ackroyd, as quickly as you can. It's nearly half-past four—'

'Yes, but what's going to happen at half-past four?' asked Rose, clasping her hands anxiously.

'Ben's goin' ter *flit*,' observed that worthy.

'I don't know what's going to happen at half-past four, Miss Ackroyd,' said Fordyce. 'Perhaps nothing. But it'll be best for you to be out of the way, anyhow, and I ask you to trust me, and to follow my advice. Go back to your house—'

'Oh!' she cried. 'But my key!'

'Eh?'

'My latch-key,' she repeated. 'I've left it behind.'

'Whew!' muttered Fordyce, whistling softly. 'That means the only way back is over the roof?'

'Yes.'

'Are you game to face it again?'

'Oh, yes. If I must. But—'

'I'll go with you, if you like.'

'Yus, and so'll I,' interposed Ben. 'Yer ain't goin' ter leave me alone in this blinkin' 'ouse, doncher think it. We'll orl flit tergether—'allo! Wot's that?'

Through the window came again the muffled chimes of the church clock. They chimed half-past four. And barely had the chimes ceased to reverberate when the front-door bell rang.

'My Gawd!' gasped Ben hysterically. 'That's done it!'

14

Half-past Four

For a moment no one moved. The bell sounded through the empty house like a ghostly challenge; and, almost immediately, the challenge was repeated, and the bell rang a second time.

Fordyce accepted the challenge. He smiled at Rose, who was leaning against the wall, with her hand at her breast, and then addressed the jibbering seaman, swiftly and sharply.

'Listen to me, Ben,' he said. 'We're up against it now. See if you can be a man for once! I'm going down to answer that bell, and until we know who it is, Miss Ackroyd must be out of the way. Have you got that clear?'

Ben made no reply.

'You say it's quite a safe journey across the roof, Miss Ackroyd?' asked Fordyce, turning to her.

'Quite—I can manage it,' she murmured faintly.

'Good! Then get across at once. But, for God's sake, be careful! Go back, and wait there till I come—I'll let you know what all this is about presently. And you, Ben—'

'Y-yus. Wot abart me?'

'You stay here, and try to work up a little pluck.'

Fordyce seized one of the candles, and made for the door.

'Oi,' muttered Ben. ''Adn't I better jest see 'er 'ome like?'

'No, old chap. I may need you presently myself. Let's see what the Merchant Service can do. You can give Miss Ackroyd a leg up the skylight, though—and then you can come down with me, if you like—'

'No, thanks, guv'nor,' said Ben shakily. 'Think I'll wait 'ere—ready like!'

The bell rang again.

'Now, then, out of the window with you, Miss Ackroyd,' whispered Fordyce. 'And—good luck!'

So saying, he ran out into the passage, and they heard him hurrying downstairs. Rose turned, and stared at Ben.

'Go hon, miss,' urged Ben. 'Hover the roof!'

'Why didn't you act like a man, and go down with him?' she demanded indignantly.

'Lummy,' thought the seaman. 'Now *she's* off!' Aloud he replied, 'Ain't got no nerve today, miss, that's a fack. Carn't be a 'ero on a hempty stummick, I ses.'

'You'll stay here, though?' she persisted. 'You'll stay here—in case he wants help?'

''E don't want no 'elp, that chap,' retorted Ben. ''Ere, why doncher pop off?'

'I don't trust you!'

'Oo's haskin' yer to? Fer the love o' Mike—nah, then, wotcher doin'?'

Rose slipped to the door quickly and closed it, and, before Ben could reach her, had turned the key and taken it out.

Then Ben saw red. What was the matter with everybody?

Did they think he was a bloomin' slave? He hadn't signed on to be everyone's servant, to go where they told him, and to stop when they commanded him. This wasn't a ship. This was a house. And he wasn't going to stand it!

And all at once, in the midst of his anger, the means of enforcing his point came to him. His hand touched his side, and came against something hard. The revolver! He'd forgotten that.

Facing Rose fiercely, he cried:

'Wotcher lock that door for?'

'To stop you from running away over the roof,' Rose retorted defiantly.

'Well—and why shouldn't I?'

'Because he told you not to.'

'Oh! And 'oo's '*e*?'

'Something you're not. A brave man!'

'I ain't brave, ain't I? Well, we'll see abart that in a minit! But wot abart you? *You* was goin' hover the roof—'

'That's just where you're wrong,' she interrupted hotly. 'I wasn't going over the roof. I was going to stay here—and I'm *going* to stay here!'

'Ye'r' potty! Why?' blazed Ben, fumbling in his pocket.

'I'll tell you!' Her voice was firm. 'There's two reasons. I'm not going to leave *him*. And I'm not going away from this house until I've found my father! There! And you aren't, either!'

'Ain't I?'

'No!'

'Think again, miss—I gives yer one more charnce.'

'What do you mean?'

'Wot I ses,' answered Ben desperately. 'Unlock that there door.'

'I won't.'

'Yer won't? Orl right, then—we'll 'ave ter see abart that!' He whipped out his revolver, and pointed it at her. She gave a gasp. '*Nah*, then, miss—will yer unlock that door?'

But Rose Ackroyd stood firm, though her eyes were round with terror.

'I won't, I won't!' she panted.

'Yer better,' said Ben hoarsely, his hand shaking. 'It might go horf!'

'I don't care!'

Didn't she? Well, Ben did. Perspiration dripped freely down his forehead. Still brandishing the revolver at her, he exclaimed:

'Look 'ere, miss, look 'ere, I ain't goin' ter 'urt yer. Not if ye'r' a sensible gal. *Ye'r'* makin' me do this, actin' like a loonertick! I ain't the murderin' sort—'

'I'm not so sure about that!' she gasped.

'I tells yer, I ain't.'

'Well, then, prove it by putting that pistol back in your pocket.'

'This ain't in my line, stright it ain't,' persisted Ben, stepping closer to her, 'but I wants ter quit, see? I've 'ad enuff o' this 'ouse. And if yer don't come away from that there door—unlock it, I mean—'

'You say murder isn't in your line,' interrupted Rose, struggling to keep calm while the revolver was pointed at her breast, 'but if you're speaking the truth, how is it you've got a revolver on you? Tell me that!'

'Eh?' blinked Ben. 'I got it orf the corpse.'

He jerked his thumb towards the adjoining room and Rose stifled a cry.

'Corpse!' she gasped, almost sobbing. 'What corpse?'

'There, that's done it,' muttered Ben, his brain growing dizzy. He lowered the revolver. 'Don't tike hon, miss. The corpse we fahnd—'

'Why—?'

'I was goin' ter tell yer, but that Nosey Parker feller kep' on chippin' in. 'E didn't give me no charnce. But it ain't yer father—don't tike hon, miss—it ain't yer father!'

'How do you know?'

''Cos I'm tellin' yer. This feller's got a crooked shoulder. So it's yer old lodger, I reckons—that Smith feller.'

Rose closed her eyes for a moment. Plucky though she was, this last minute had almost taxed her beyond endurance. She reopened her eyes quickly, however, at an exclamation from Ben.

'Oi!' he muttered. 'Wot was that?'

'It was a door slamming,' answered Rose, in a low voice. 'They're coming up.'

'They? 'Oo?'

'We'll know soon. The police, I hope.'

'Lor, lummy,' chattered Ben. 'S'pose it *is* the perlice?'

'Well—have you any need to be afraid of them?' she asked sharply.

'Me? No! But—'

'But you *are* afraid! And when they find you with that revolver on you—'

'Swipe me!' exclaimed Ben. 'I better put it back! Yus, that's wot I'll do—I'll put it back!'

With a despairing gesture, he rushed to the door leading to the inner room, fumbled with the key, unlocked it, and dived in. A second later, he fell back with a gasp of terror.

''Oly Moses!' he choked. ''E's gorn!'

15

The House-Hunters

There was no time to probe into this astonishing new development before another matter, of equal moment, claimed the bewildered couple's attention. Footsteps were ascending the stairs outside, and the foremost had already reached the landing. Instinctively, Rose slipped to the passage door and unlocked it, while Ben quickly closed the door leading to the inner chamber.

Then the door from the passage opened, and Fordyce appeared. Surprised to find Rose still in the room, he concealed his surprise well, merely remarking casually, for the benefit of three dim figures behind him:

'Oh—you still here?'

'Yes,' answered Rose faintly. 'I—thought I'd wait.'

Fordyce nodded. Something had happened, obviously, but this was not the opportunity to ask questions. Recovering himself quickly from his last traces of uncertainty, he remarked, in a natural voice:

'Some people have come to look over the house. You'll

excuse us a moment, won't you? They—er—insist on seeing every room. Come in, won't you?'

The three figures behind him entered. One was an elderly, well-dressed man, but with a rough, common atmosphere about him which he did his best to hide. He was clean-shaven, with quickly moving, ferret-like eyes. At the moment, they were roving restlessly. In fact, their owner appeared to be suffering from a thinly concealed attack of nerves.

Of the two other members of the party, one was a youth, the other a girl. The youth was tall, and presented a somewhat odd appearance. His eyes also roved about, but not with any weight of responsibility; he looked, in truth, like a simpleton, and when he spoke he contributed further to that impression. One might have set him down as a youth whose body had grown while his brain had dwindled.

The girl was likewise tall, but in that fact alone did she resemble the youth. She was extremely beautiful, and behind her present rather bored exterior a keen brain worked. She smiled faintly at Fordyce, as he invited them in, and she explained their insistence on seeing over the whole house half-apologetically, half-cynically.

'That's my brother's fault, I'm afraid. Henry's so particular,' she said. 'I'm quite sure *I* didn't want to climb all these stairs.'

Fordyce looked at her curiously.

'No?' he queried. 'Well, I did my best to dissuade you, didn't I?'

She flushed slightly under his scrutiny. There was something besides curiosity in Fordyce's gaze. While she turned away, and regarded the peeling walls, the youth whom she had referred to as Henry, her brother, carried on the conversation.

'Well,' he remarked, in a simple voice, 'one can't be too careful, I always think. One's got to be careful. Hasn't one? You remember, Nora, don't you, that time we took a house, and then, after we'd taken it, all the ceilings leaked? Why, the first wet day—'

The elderly man interposed, irritably.

'Yes, yes, my boy—best see everything, of course,' he exclaimed. 'But perhaps if you'd see a little more and talk a little less, we'd get on faster!'

'Oh, sorry, Uncle,' murmured the youth. 'But—'

'Be quiet!' snapped the elderly man, and turned to Fordyce. 'Er—now then. What's this? Cupboard?'

'Yes, cupboard,' answered Fordyce, professionally.

'H'm. Keep it locked, I see.'

'That's easily remedied.' Fordyce unlocked and unbolted the cupboard, displaying its interior. 'Nice roomy cupboard, isn't it?'

The elderly man shot a glance into it, and then looked sharply at Fordyce.

'Wigs, eh?' he remarked.

'Yes. Wigs and cobwebs,' nodded Fordyce.

'Ah. In the theatre business?'

'Not personally. I imagine, though, that the last tenant must have been in the amateur line.' There was a short pause. No one appeared to know quite what to say next. 'It *is* rather a remarkable cupboard, isn't it?' said Fordyce coolly.

Nora answered him, with equal coolness.

'Yes, the cupboards are certainly good in this house, but frankly I can't say much for anything else. Don't you think, Uncle,' she added, turning to the elderly man, who was fidgeting from one foot to the other, 'don't you think we'd better go now, and think it over?'

Henry began to wander towards the fireplace, holding out his hands to the fire. 'Cupboards are very useful things,' he remarked vapidly. 'I always think they're as important as anything. Do you remember, Nora, that cupboard we used to hide the jam in?'

'Oh, do hold that tongue of yours, my boy!' cried the elderly man. 'This isn't the time for reminiscences!' He pointed to the door by the fireplace. 'Is that another room in there?'

Fordyce answered airily, but keeping a careful watch:

'Yes, but it's in no sort of condition at the moment. It's just like this one.'

'I think we might have to look at it, just the same, if you've no objection?'

'Yes, you remember those ceilings,' added Henry, tapping his nose.

Moving a step nearer the door as he spoke, Fordyce replied lightly:

'Oh, I assure you, you needn't worry about the ceilings in this house. The ceilings are all right. Perfectly watertight.'

A train rumbled beneath and the vibration brought another little shower of plaster from the ceiling to the floor. Under cover of the incident, Henry slipped a hand on the mantelpiece, and conveyed the handcuffs that had been lying there to his pocket. This was not quite the action of a simpleton. 'And now, Mr—,' began Fordyce, and paused. 'By the way, I don't think you've told me your name yet?'

'Eh? Oh, Brant,' replied the elderly man. 'Brant.'

'Thank you. And may I know yours, too?'

The remark was addressed to Henry.

'Mine? Oh, same as his. Henry Brant. And that's my sister, Nora. All in the family.'

'Yes, that's right,' interposed Brant. 'And now, perhaps, we might ask *your* name?'

The tone was slightly insolent, but Fordyce affected not to notice it.

'My name? Why, certainly,' he said pleasantly. 'But surely the agent told you?'

'Of course he did,' replied Brant, slightly flustered. 'Yes, of course. But I've a bad memory for names. Haven't I, my dear?' He turned to Nora for corroboration. 'Let's see—it wasn't Barnaby, was it?'

'No,' answered Fordyce, smiling rather ironically. 'It wasn't Barnaby.'

'That was the name of the last man we saw, Uncle,' interposed Nora quickly. 'How stupid of you!'

'Well, at any rate,' pressed Fordyce, 'you remember the name of the agent who sent you here?'

'Eh?' jerked Brant.

'Aren't we wasting time?' suggested Nora, frowning.

'No, I don't think so,' Fordyce assured them. 'I *should* like to know which agent you came from. He ought to have given you an order to view. They're such sharpers, you know.'

'Oh, Jones, I think,' exclaimed Brant irritably. 'As my niece says, what's it matter? How can one remember, anyway? There are so many.'

'Oh, you mean Johns,' said Fordyce, catching at the name.

'Ah—Johns. That's the man,' nodded Brant.

'Johns, of Grindle Street?'

'Yes, Grindle Street.'

'Next to the post-office?'

'That's it.'

Fordyce paused, and turned suddenly to Rose.

'I wonder if you'd mind leaving us for a few minutes?' he asked. 'We've just a little business to discuss.'

Before Rose could answer, Nora interposed.

'I really don't think there's any business to discuss at all,' she said icily.

'Well, I think there is,' answered Fordyce. 'I know another place you might like to live in, if this place doesn't suit. The ceilings are quite secure there—and the door.'

''Ear, 'ear,' murmured Ben softly.

Fordyce turned to Rose again. 'What do you think? Perhaps you'd better be getting home. I may be some little time. I'll see you later, of course.'

'Oh, she don't live here, then?' inquired Brant, with a swift glance at Rose.

'No,' answered Fordyce shortly. 'The house isn't exactly furnished for residential purposes.'

'Well, caretakers, you know,' growled Brant. 'There might have been a room somewhere. And what about *him*?'

He jerked his head towards Ben, and Fordyce frowned severely.

'Aren't you a trifle curious about my private affairs?' he demanded. 'It isn't quite usual, you know, to discuss these things with house-hunters.'

'Oh, I beg your pardon, I'm sure—'

'Not at all. If you really want to know, this is my servant, Ben—'

'Yus, that's me,' nodded Ben emphatically.

'And this'—Fordyce indicated Rose—'is a little friend of mine. Now, run away, will you, as I said?'

Rose looked at him, hesitatingly. Then she walked to the door. But, before she slipped out, she gazed directly at Fordyce, and said:

'As you think it's best. But—I won't leave the house!'

She smiled as she departed, and Fordyce smiled back at her. His smile changed rapidly to a frown, however, when he turned and saw Henry moving towards the door to the inner room.

'Now, then, not so fast, young man!' he exclaimed, interposing. 'This house isn't yours yet, you know!'

'But we're thinking of taking it, aren't we?' replied Henry blandly. 'And so I was just thinking of looking in there.'

The two men regarded each other fixedly. In the short silence that followed, two wills combated.

'Tell me then,' said Fordyce—'just as a matter of curiosity. Why are you so particularly keen to see that room?'

'Well, if you want to know,' responded Henry promptly, 'it's because you're so particularly keen not to show it to me. Funny how we're made, isn't it?'

Fordyce smiled. And, suddenly, Ben rubbed his eyes and stared at Henry. Where had he seen him before? . . .

'Now, I call that a perfectly sound reason,' observed Fordyce. 'I'm rather built that way myself. When people hide things from me, I simply can't rest till I know what they're keeping back.'

'And there's somethink familier abart them hother two,' thought Ben. 'But I'll swear I ain't seed *them* afore . . .'

Fordyce was still speaking.

'If you like, I'll return frankness for frankness. The reason why I don't feel under any further obligation to show you any more rooms is because I am perfectly certain you have no intention of taking this house.'

'I think I have already implied as much,' answered Nora frigidly, while her uncle muttered, 'Impudence!'

'And I am equally certain,' continued Fordyce, 'that you never had any intention of taking this house.'

'Confound you, sir—' began Brant.

'When I opened the front door to you just now, you seemed surprised to see me. Perhaps you expected to see someone else? If that young gentleman there,' added Fordyce, glancing at Henry, 'who is so curious about the ceilings and who affects to be so deficient in the top storey himself, had not stuck his foot very definitely in the doorway, I think you other two would have fled. But he insisted on coming in—and, having come in, you all stuck to your parts.'

Brant started to bluster.

'Our parts?' he exclaimed. 'Our parts? What do you mean? What the devil do you take us for?'

'Well, not for house-hunters, certainly,' replied Fordyce calmly. 'It may interest you to know that there is no such agent as Johns, of Grindle Street.'

'Bah!'

'There isn't such a street as Grindle Street. I invented it.'

For a second, Brant was speechless. Henry smiled quietly, and it was Nora who tried to save the situation. She did not attempt the impossible feat of trying to rebuild the structure which Fordyce's trick had toppled to the ground. She merely walked to the door, observing:

'All this is quite profitless. Let's be going.'

''Ear, 'ear,' cheered Ben.

Brant fumed with righteous indignation, or with indignation which he tried to make appear righteous.

'Monstrous! Scandalous!' he cried. 'I never heard

anything like it! Not house-hunters, eh? Well, for that matter, are you a house-owner?'

'I don't see any necessity to inform you,' responded Fordyce.

'No? Well, that's interesting,' said Brant, looking at his companions for corroboration and support. 'Very interesting. But suppose—I insist?'

'Insist?' frowned Fordyce.

'Yes, insist!' He advanced a step towards Fordyce, threateningly.

'Careful!' warned Nora, at the door.

'Silence, Nora! This man's an impudent—'

''Ere, 'ere!' interposed Ben, suddenly stepping forward. 'None o' yer sorse, guv'nor!'

'Sauce!' fumed Brant, turning on him savagely.

'Yus, sorse! S-o-r-s, sorse! That's wot I ses. None o' yer—'

'Don't interfere, Ben,' interrupted Fordyce. 'Leave this to me.'

But Ben was working up. The tides of courage and indignation were rising, encouraged by what he conceived to be the weaknesses of his opponents. He could tell them a thing or two. He could *show* them a thing or two! If all else failed, he had something useful still in his pocket.

'I begs ter differ, guv'nor, as they ses in perlite society,' he replied to Fordyce. 'Let 'em *go* hin the nex' room and 'ave a look, if they wants ter.' He swung round to Brant. 'Go hin, Nosey Parker! Look till ye'r' blind!'

'Are you mad, Ben?' exclaimed Fordyce.

'No, I ain't,' retorted Ben excitedly, 'and I tike some credit fer that!'

'What an amusing man!' murmured Nora, while the others hesitated.

'Yus—reg'ler George Robey, ain't I? Well—wotcher waitin' for? Yer was nosey enuff afore the hinvite came! They won't find nothink. They won't find no leakin' roof—no, *hor* no leakin' body!'

'Body!' cried Brant, while the others started.

'You fool!' growled Fordyce helplessly.

'Wotcher waitin' for?' roared Ben. 'Shall I call yer a taxi?'

'No, thanks—I'll walk,' said Henry suddenly, and, opening the door, entered the room.

Fordyce stared at Ben. Then he followed Henry. In the tense silence that followed, Brant drew nearer to Nora, and whispered to her. Then they fastened their eyes on the doorway, and, a second later, Henry came out, followed by Fordyce, the latter's face wearing a look of blank astonishment.

'Nothing remarkable in there,' commented Henry.

'Wot did I say?' retorted Ben. 'Roof leakin', ducky? That's orl right, then. Nah I s'pose yer'll tike the 'ouse. Well, yer can 'ave it, fer I ain't makin' no hoffers. I'm goin'!'

He made a movement towards the passage, but Brant intruded his agitated form.

'Not so fast, my man—not so fast!' he exclaimed.

'Fast, is it?' cried Ben, growing more and more excited, and realising that, once he allowed his spirit to drop, he was done for. 'Oh, I'm a little flash o' lightnin', I am! I've bin tryin' ter move hout o' this bloomin' 'ouse fer a hour, and I've moved 'arf-a-hinch. Real Derby winner, ain't I? Nah, then, git hout of it!'

He gave Brant a thrust, but Brant thrust him back. The next moment, Ben whipped out his revolver.

'Orl right, yer *will* 'ave it!' he shouted fiercely. ''Ands hup!'

A gasp of astonishment went round the room. Brant, although covered, did not move, as though unable to credit the fact that this dilapidated seaman could really constitute a menace.

'Where on earth did you get that?' cried Fordyce, in one last effort to stem the tide.

'Orf the corpse—'

'Corpse!' blinked Brant.

'There, that's done it, but it don't matter. It ain't nothink ter do with me. *'E* knows that. And I'm goin' ter 'op it. Yus, and if hennybody hinterferes, there'll be more corpses, see? Lor' blimy, yus!'

Fordyce advanced resolutely to Ben.

'Put that down,' he said, very sternly. 'Put it down, do you hear? You're the biggest dolt I've ever come across, and you'll hang yourself yet. It's true,' he said, to the others, 'there *was* a dead man in the next room, and I was on the point of calling the police when you arrived.' He turned back to Ben, who was still brandishing the revolver. 'What's happened, Ben? Have you done anything?'

Ben's voice now rose to a frenzy.

'Me done hennythink?' he cried wildly. 'That's right, guv'nor—blime the 'ole bloomin' war onter me! 'Corse I ain't done nothink. Yer doesn't need to do things in this' 'ere 'ouse. Yer jest stands still, and they 'appen. Everythink's looney. People comin' 'ere and bein' murdered, and then 'oppin' horf agin, and footsteps without no feet, and then *you* comin' 'ere and givin' nimes of 'ouse agents wot don't hexist—swipe me, I'm fair sick ter death of it, stright. And I'm goin', and I'll send the perlice back 'ere right enuff, don't you worry. Git hout o' my way!'

Fordyce made a grab at him, but, for once, Ben was

too quick, and darted aside. Then Nora began to walk forward.

'Come, don't be foolish,' she said quietly. 'Give me that revolver.'

'Keep orf, keep orf,' shouted Ben.

'Be careful,' warned Fordyce.

But Nora kept on. 'Give it to me,' she said, and stretched out her hand.

'Keep orf, I say!' yelled Ben, brandishing the revolver wildly.

'Look out, Ben!' cried Fordyce suddenly.

For now Brant and Henry had whipped out revolvers, and their attitudes denoted that they meant business. Ben saw them, and lost his head utterly. Leaping forward just before Ben's frantic shot rang out, Fordyce hurled himself in front of Nora—and, the next instant, nearly doubled up.

'Guv'nor!' gasped Ben. 'Guv'nor—!'

Sobered, he dropped his pistol.

16

Cross-Examination

Henry darted forward and picked up Ben's revolver. He no longer wore the look of a simpleton. Indeed, although Brant now took charge of the situation, Henry was the cooler of the two, and followed events with more quiet assurance.

Nora, like Ben, was momentarily dazed. She watched Gilbert Fordyce slowly straighten from his sudden spasm of pain, and, as he spoke, a look of intense relief spread over her face.

'Well—that's that,' muttered Fordyce.

'Guv'nor!' stammered the seaman contritely. 'I didn't mean it—yer knows that. I never knowed it was loaded.'

'It's just as well to find out first, you know,' replied Fordyce, gritting his teeth. 'But don't worry, Ben. It's only a graze.'

He took a handkerchief from his pocket with his left hand, and dropped it over his right wrist. Nora sprang forward.

'Can I—can I—?' she asked.

'Ah, may I trouble you?' asked Fordyce coolly.

She took the handkerchief, examined the wound, and bound the handkerchief round it. As he had said, it was only a graze, but it might have been considerably more. Nora shuddered—an odd thing, perhaps, for such a cool young lady to do.

'That was rather—decent of you,' she murmured.

'A pity it couldn't have been in a slightly better cause, eh?' suggested Fordyce.

Nora bit her lip. 'Perhaps we can't all be choosers, you know.'

He shot a quick glance at her.

'Do you mean that?'

She answered his glance, but not his question.

'Is that too tight?' she inquired.

'No,' said Fordyce. 'Just right. Thanks.'

The passage door swung open, and Rose came running in. She had heard the shot and her eyes were wide with fear, a fear that did not decrease when she saw Fordyce's bound wrist, and the threatening revolvers of the two male 'house-hunters.' Henry was standing over Ben, and Brant now swung round quickly to her.

'What was that?' she cried.

'Ah, come in, you!' retorted Brant sharply. 'Now you've come back, you can stay back, till I've cleared this up a bit.' She hesitated, and he repeated, angrily, 'Come in! D'you hear?'

He advanced to her, as she stood cowering by the door, and seized her shoulder. Fordyce glared at him.

'Don't you treat her roughly,' he growled.

'Be quiet!' Brant snapped back, and giving the girl a shove, said, 'Get over there.'

'What's happened?' gasped Rose.

'Never you mind,' answered Brant. 'You speak when I ask you to—not till then. Now then, you,' he cried, turning back to Fordyce, 'put 'em up!'

'Sorry,' responded Fordyce calmly, 'but I've got a better use for them.'

His hand moved towards his pocket, and Brant barked quickly:

'Now then—none of that! Keep your hand out of your pocket, or—'

'You don't mind if I smoke, do you?' queried Fordyce, bringing out his cigarette case.

'Yes, I do,' retorted Brant angrily.

'That's unfortunate,' murmured Fordyce as he opened the case and extracted a cigarette.

'You're running yourself into danger,' Brant warned him.

'Oh, I'm in no danger,' observed Fordyce. 'You see, the hangman won't worry if I smoke. But he might—if you shoot.'

A red flush began to spread over Brant's countenance, and he wavered.

'Uncle!' warned Nora.

'Oh—bah!' fumed Brant. 'Well, get on with it. Search him, my boy,' he said to Henry. 'I'll see he doesn't get up to any mischief.'

'Righto,' replied Henry briskly. 'Yes, give him a bullet if he tries to knock me on the head!'

The first article he took out of Fordyce's pocket was a box of matches. Fordyce relieved him of the box, smilingly.

'Thanks, just what I wanted,' he remarked, and lit his cigarette. Then he returned the case to Henry.

'Cool, aren't you?' said Henry.

'You're not so bad yourself,' replied Fordyce. 'Rather a handsome case, isn't it?'

Henry read out the initials, 'G. F.,' and Ben smiled faintly.

'Yus, I knows wot that stands for,' he muttered.

Henry completed his search quickly. He was no bungler. In cash, Fordyce had only a few shillings on him. In other respects, his pockets were equally unexciting.

'Clean slate,' reported Henry.

'Good,' answered Brant. 'And, now, the other.'

Henry turned to the seaman. 'Come along, Ben,' he smiled. 'Let's see your treasures. Have you got any more little revolvers about you?'

'Nah, then,' retorted the seaman. ''Oo sed yer could call me Ben?'

'I'm sorry, I'm sure,' grinned Henry, 'but I don't know your other name.'

'Lloyd George.'

Fordyce laughed.

'You know, I like you, Ben, upon my soul I do!' he said.

'Yus, I've noticed it,' answered Ben, as Henry began to examine his unilluminating pockets. 'I'll give yer a job in the cabbynet nex' eleckshun.'

'Thanks. What'll it be?'

''Ead o' the Messin' Abart Department. That's wot yer was born for, I reckons . . . Hout comes orl me little 'eirlooms! Nice bit o' string, 'Enery, ain't it? I've 'ad a big hoffer fer that. 'Undred pahnds—but I wouldn't tike it. Sending it ter Christie's. Hexpeck there'll be some big biddin' among the 'angmen.'

'Oh, shut that fellow's mouth!' exclaimed Brant.

'Believe me,' Fordyce assured him, 'it can't be done. I've tried myself.'

'Have you? Well, p'r'aps your methods aren't mine. Now then, Henry, haven't you finished?'

'Yes,' nodded Henry. 'Another clean slate—'

'Fust time hennybody's called me clean,' interposed Ben. 'I'm gettin' hon, I am!'

'Now the girl,' said Brant, ignoring him. 'And, for God's sake, hurry!'

Rose shrank away as Henry approached.

'Don't worry—I'm not going to hurt you,' Henry promised, and proceeded to search her quietly while Brant turned to Fordyce.

'I reckon that's a pretty story you've put up,' he exclaimed, 'but I want the truth this time. Who are you?'

'That's not your business,' answered Fordyce.

'That's where you're wrong. It *is* my business, and the sooner you get that into your head, the better for everyone. Who are you, and who's that blithering idiot over there?'

'Isn't this all rather useless, Uncle?' suggested Nora.

'Useless? We've got to get to the bottom of it, haven't we?'

'Yes, but will it help us to—' She lowered her voice. 'To get through—'

'Sh!' warned Brant. 'Perhaps the girl can tell us something.'

He turned towards her, and, as he did so, saw Henry reading the telegram which he had taken from Rose's pocket.

'Hallo—what's that?' he demanded.

'What's what?' said Henry.

'Telegram, isn't it?'

'Yes. You're in a hurry, aren't you? I was just going to read it out.'

'Were you?' answered Brant, looking at him shrewdly.

'Well, I'll save you the trouble.' He snatched the form from Henry's hand, and read: '"Keep clear No. 17 today—"'

'Ah, some 'un was wise,' murmured Ben.

'"Sheldrake moving,"' continued Brant, in a puzzled voice. '"Lie low till instructions. Suffolk necklace"—what's this?—"Suffolk necklace has been found. Barton." Barton!'

He paused, and Henry emitted a low whistle. There was a short silence, during which Rose glanced appealingly at Fordyce, and he threw her a reassuring smile. It was little enough he could do, but a smile of hope sometimes goes a long way.

'So—Detective Barton's on this game!' murmured Nora.

'Looks like it,' said Brant uneasily.

'Who's the telegram addressed to, Uncle?' she asked.

'Ackroyd,' replied Brant. 'No. 15—next door.' He barked at Rose. 'You! Where did you get this?'

'It came for my father,' answered Rose.

'Your father, eh?'

'Yes.'

'Then you're Miss Ackroyd?'

'Yes.'

'H'm. How did you get here?' Rose was silent. 'Come, answer me,' he exclaimed, in a bullying tone.

'Don't bully that girl!' cried Fordyce angrily, and turned to Nora. 'I say, Miss Brant, do you stand for this?'

'If your friend is sensible, she won't be hurt—I'll stand for that.'

'Oh, why don't they keep quiet!' burst out Brant, to the ceiling. 'Get into that next room, G. F., or whatever you call yourself, and take that blithering idiot of a friend of yours with you.' He pointed to Ben. 'Where did you get him? In a rag and bone sale? Go on—I'll call you when I want you.' Fordyce did not move. 'Step lively, now—unless you want another bullet?'

'You are a blusterer,' responded Fordyce.

'Oh! Blusterer, am I!'

Rose interposed, with a sharp little cry.

'Please go,' she said. 'They wouldn't dare hurt me—I'm sure they wouldn't.'

Fordyce frowned, and looked at Nora.

'Is that your advice, Miss Brant?' he asked.

'Yes,' she nodded. 'You'd better go. I've told you she won't be hurt.'

'That's a promise?' She nodded. 'Oh, well, come along, Ben. We're under orders—for the moment. Not permanently, you know. And cheer up, Miss Ackroyd—the fog'll pass.'

'Yes, I'm sure it will,' she replied faintly.

Ben gazed towards the door to the inner chamber uneasily.

'Wot do they wanter git rid of us for?' he demanded, as he hesitated.

'They don't like us, Ben.'

'Well, that's mewchel, ain't it? We ain't ezackly gorn on them!'

'*Will* you go?' shouted Brant.

'Oh, hennythink ter hoblige, I'm sure. Keep yer 'air hon. 'Ouse-'unter, I don't think!' He turned once more to Fordyce. 'Guv'nor, 'ave we *really* gotter go in there?'

'Afraid so, old sport.'

'Wot—in that there vanishin'-room? Well—p'r'aps *we* can do a bit o' vanishin'!'

Fordyce walked up to him, and patted him on the shoulder.

'Buck up,' he said. 'I thought you were getting back your pluck!'

'It comes and goes, like,' murmured Ben.

They went to the door. As they reached it, Fordyce turned to Brant.

'I warn you,' he remarked quietly, 'if you hurt a hair of that girl's head, there won't be a whole bone of you left to bury.'

'Which I 'opes is termorrer,' added Ben, as Fordyce swung the door open. 'No flahers, by request!'

Then they vanished into the vanishing-room, and the door closed behind them.

17

Trapped!

Brant gave a sigh of relief, and turned to Rose briskly.

'Now then,' he began, 'we can move a little faster. How did *you* get here?'

'If you want to know,' answered Rose, with a note of defiance in her voice, 'I—I came over the roof.'

'Over the roof, eh?' exclaimed Brant, with a rapid glance at the others. 'Well, that's a bit rum, isn't it?'

'Why did you come?' asked Nora.

Rose turned to her immediately, as the preferable tormentor.

'I came to find my father.'

'So!' observed Brant, whistling softly. 'Your father. And he came over first, then, eh?' He rubbed his forehead. 'Look here, my girl. That man whose body's supposed to have been in the next room—was *that* your father?'

'No, thank God!' exclaimed Rose.

'Yes, yes, but are you quite sure? Did you see him?'

'No,' answered Rose faintly.

'Very well, then! How do you *know* it wasn't your father? It might have been.'

'Don't be so brutal!' murmured Nora.

'I tell you, it wasn't,' exclaimed Rose, all the more emphatic because of her sudden doubt. 'They said it was—a man who used to lodge with us a little while ago.'

'What was his name?'

'Smith.'

Once more Brant glanced at the others significantly. His eyes rested for a moment on Henry, who was sitting quietly on a case, silent and listening. He returned to Rose.

'His name was Smith. Well, that's a common name enough, isn't it? Might be anybody, mightn't it? But what would this Mr Smith be doing here?'

'I don't know,' replied Rose, shaking her head wearily. 'It's no good asking me that.'

'Well, I'll ask you this, then. Was there any trouble between this Mr Smith and your father?'

'No!' answered Rose, very decisively.

'You seem very certain?'

'I am certain!' She knew what they were trying to make out. Her eyes flashed with indignation.

'Well, well, my girl, I've not denied it yet, have I? But, look here, let's straighten this out a bit more. *You* came across the roof after your father—'

'Yes.'

'But why did *he* come across?'

'I don't know.'

'Don't? Or won't?' Suddenly he shot out, 'That telegram! Did he know anything about that?'

'No. It came after he'd gone.'

'After he'd gone! Then—he never got it?'

'No.'

'The warning missed him,' Brant muttered. 'Well, then, what about those diamonds?'

'I don't know.'

'Damn it, you don't know anything—!'

'Hush! You frighten her!' interposed Nora. 'Let me go on with this. Tell us, Miss Ackroyd, are you in your father's confidence?'

'In his confidence?' repeated Rose. 'What do you mean?'

'Well, mightn't your father have some secret he's keeping from you? Connected, you know, with Mr Smith—and the way over the roof?'

Rose's mind began to spin. She did not answer. With a half-triumphant glance at his niece, Brant resumed the attack.

'This Mr Smith, now,' he said. 'You spoke of him as a lodger you *used* to have. When did he leave?'

'He left us six months ago.'

'Six—months—ago!' repeated Brant slowly. The information appeared to astonish him considerably, and he made little effort to conceal his surprise, in spite of his niece's warning signs. 'You say Mr Smith left you six months ago. Why did he leave? Come, *why* did he leave?'

Rose began to grow hysterical.

'Why did he leave?' she cried. 'Why are *you* asking me all these questions?'

'Because—'

'If you ask me anything more, I shall scream!'

Nora laid her arm on her uncle's sleeve. 'Better go slow, I think,' she said. 'She's about reached the end of herself.'

'Yes, you're right,' muttered Brant grudgingly. 'Look here, Miss Ackroyd, I've finished with you—for the present. Go into that room and send me that fellow they call Ben. Now, then, hurry up!'

Rose walked mechanically to the door, Brant following her. Then Henry broke his long silence, and addressed a remark to Nora behind her uncle's back.

'Never get anywhere at this game, he won't,' he murmured. 'All nerves.'

Rose opened the door, and passed unsteadily into the inner room. When it was closed, Brant turned round, and faced his companions with a deep frown.

'Rum go, isn't it?' observed Henry.

'Rum? It's a double-cross!' rasped Brant. 'Damn it, call this a get-away? It looks more like being a put-away! If Smith hasn't been here for six months, we're being double-crossed, to a certainty!'

Alone now, their tongues were loosened; yet, even so, there was a strange atmosphere of suspicion in that gloomy room. United against the three people in that inner chamber, they did not appear united among themselves.

Brant scowled at Henry, who smiled blandly back. Nora frowned at both.

'It looks to me,' she observed, with a shrug, 'as if Ackroyd's been carrying on Smith's game.'

'He must have been,' Henry nodded. 'Confoundedly clever of him—'

'I said it was madness to come in here,' interrupted Brant, clenching his hand impotently. 'Didn't I? Didn't I, Nora?'

'It's what I've been saying all along,' retorted Nora. 'We ought to have made some excuse on the doorstep.'

'Well, I wanted to,' said Brant angrily, 'only our precious Henry wouldn't let us.'

'Well, even after that,' Nora went on, 'we could have gone, without wasting all this useless time. We can go now!'

'Can we, my dear Nora?' queried Henry. 'I'm not quite sure of that.'

Brant turned on him savagely.

'There you go—putting your confounded spoke in again,' he exclaimed. 'Who the devil are you, anyway?'

'A brother in misfortune,' responded Henry smoothly. 'Isn't that enough?'

'Not quite, Henry,' answered Nora, as smoothly. 'We'd like to know who you *really* are?'

'What a question, from a sister!' observed Henry sarcastically. 'I'm your brother, my child, by adoption, on the doorstep—'

'Oh, don't be funny,' interposed Brant. 'We know you butted in on the doorstep. But what are you after? That's something we *don't* know!'

'Oh, don't lose your wool,' returned Henry, changing his tone. 'I'm after Smith, the same as you are. This is the Get-Away Guild, isn't it? Very well then. I'm *here* to get away. They've had a large enough slice of my plunder, and it's about time I saw some return for it.'

'Ah, that's what we say,' agreed Brant, with a glance at Nora. 'So you've got to slip the country, too?'

'Yes, damn quick. I'm here for Smith and his blasted tunnel—and Smith isn't here to show us the way! I've got my appointment card, same as you have—4.30 appointment for the Goods Train Ferry for the Continent, that starts under this house. Satisfied yet, or not?' he added. 'Here's my ticket. Where's yours?'

He whipped a little badge out of his pocket inscribed,

'No. 17. 4.30.' Brant and Nora produced theirs. Brant nodded, satisfied, but Nora regarded Henry dubiously.

'Are you quite sure that's *your* ticket, Henry?' she asked.

'Of course it's my ticket,' answered Henry. 'What do you mean?'

Nora hesitated, then responded:

'Well, I saw it in your hand when you took the telegram from Miss Ackroyd's pocket.'

'Perfectly true, cute one! I was keeping it handy. Anything wrong in that?'

Brant frowned, his doubts beginning to return. He asked, suspiciously:

'Let's hear—what are *you* wanted for?'

'Gawd knows,' said a voice behind him. 'Didn't yer send fer me?'

Ben had just popped his reluctant head in from the adjoining room. He had taken his time, being in no hurry for an interview which promised little pleasantness. And, now he had appeared, he discovered he was too soon.

'Not yet, you fool!' shouted Brant.

'Oh! Wrong agin,' muttered Ben, and popped his head back once more.

'That fellow's the biggest fool!' grumbled Brant irritably.

'And so are you, Uncle,' said Nora severely, 'raising your voice like that. You're losing your nerve. Bullies are always cowards!'

'Pah! What's come over her?' murmured Brant, angry because of the truth of her words. He was losing his nerve, and he knew it. He fastened on Henry again. 'One of the queerest things about the whole business is that telegram. Those Suffolk diamonds, now—do you know anything about them? Were you in that scoop?'

'Why should I be?' answered Henry. 'That was Sheldrake's job. Don't you remember?'

'Yes, I know. And—so the telegram says—Sheldrake's moving! What the devil's that mean? Sheldrake was gaoled for it six months ago—'

'But they never found the diamonds.'

'No. I know that.'

'He'd hidden them too well.'

'Exactly. And Barton—who's sent this wire—is supposed to have sworn to find 'em. All right. I reckon I'm as well up in the history of these things as you are. But I don't understand how Sheldrake can be moving, if he's in prison—'

'Ah, that's because you're *not* quite as well up in the history of these things as I am,' interposed Henry, smiling quietly. 'You didn't know, for instance, that Sheldrake broke prison last week.'

Brant stared at him, and so did Nora.

'What!' he exclaimed. 'Did he, by God!' Henry nodded. A sudden panic seized Brant. 'Well, then, the thing's clear, isn't it? Sheldrake knows this place—he's bound to know it—bound to know Smith, and I'll bet he's heading for this get-away—'

'Yes, and with Barton after him!' interposed Nora suddenly.

Brant nodded despairingly.

'There you are! That's what I mean! By God, if Barton's making for here, we're done for.'

'Oh, you give up at every point,' cried Nora scornfully. 'There's one way open still.'

'What?'

'The way I've urged all along. The way out. What about a bolt for the front door—*now*?'

'Yes, yes!'—agreed Brant excitedly. 'That's the only thing. We won't worry about them in there. Come along my girl, come along—'

He threw open the passage door, and then stopped suddenly.

The front-door bell was ringing.

18

The Unseen Figure

For the first time since he had entered that room, Henry looked anxious. The uncanniness of the house, which had gripped each other inmate in turn, appeared to have left him cold; but now, as the bell sounded in their ears, something of his coolness left him, and a startled expression entered his eyes.

'Damn,' he muttered softly, and for five seconds no other word was spoken.

Then Brant, unable to stand the silence any longer, chattered:

'Suppose—that's Barton, and the police!'

'Keep your head!' answered Nora. 'It might be anybody.'

'Who could it be—if it's not the police?' insisted Brant shakily.

Nora looked at Henry, as she replied:

'It might be—Sheldrake?'

Henry nodded, and regained command of himself.

'Cute kid,' he said. 'That's far more likely!' He paused, then suddenly added, 'I say! If it *is* Sheldrake—are we going to let him get clear with all those diamonds? Fair's fair, eh?—when the odds are three to one against him. Eh?'

'Hallo—that's an idea, certainly,' answered Brant, licking his lips.

'It *is* an idea. What do you say to making him divide? It's £40,000. Worth just a little bit of trouble, eh?'

'By God, yes!'

'Fools,' snorted Nora. 'Shoot your lion first—then think about sharing the carcase!'

'Don't listen to her,' interposed Brant. 'Yes, it's a big deal. We'll—'

Again the bell rang, its note vibrating hollowly through the house. Brant took out his handkerchief, and wiped his forehead. He glanced at Henry.

'Er—well,' he muttered. 'Who's going down?'

Henry smiled grimly. 'I'm sure you'd make an excellent butler,' he observed, with irony.

'Nonsense! Nonsense! This isn't the time to . . . You go, Nora.'

'No, hold on,' interrupted Henry suddenly. 'I've an idea. There's a window on the next landing—I may get a squint who it is from there.'

He darted from the room, and disappeared down the rickety stairs. Nora drew nearer to her uncle as soon as they were alone, and spoke in a lowered voice.

'Keep your head, Uncle,' she whispered. 'And—watch *him*!'

'I am watching him,' answered Brant testily. 'But what do you mean?'

'Don't trust him. That's what I mean. That wasn't his badge he showed us. He took it off the Ackroyd girl—'

'What?'

'It's true. I saw him.'

'You did? My God! Then perhaps—' He seized her arm in a tight grip. 'Perhaps *he's* Sheldrake!'

'I thought of that. But perhaps he's anybody! There's no one you can trust in this crooked life—this life you've tricked me into!' she burst out impulsively.

Brant snapped his teeth. 'I do wish you'd shut up that sort of talk,' he complained. 'This isn't the time for it. We've got to find Smith and his damned tunnel. We'll talk when we get to The Hague—'

'You're an optimist,' remarked Nora. 'It's a quality I've not noticed in you before. How shall we get to The Hague if Smith is dead?'

'Yes, but how do we *know* he's dead?' Brant rapped back. 'Is he? If he's dead, where's his body? There you are . . . Confound that fellow downstairs! Why doesn't he come up again? . . . As I was saying—where's his body? I don't believe he *is* dead. But that's the thing we've got to find out. Come on—we'll have that sailor in.' He ran towards the door of the inner room. 'Yes, I'll tickle him up a bit!'

But Nora was swiftly by his side, looking straight into his eyes.

'Uncle,' she said, 'I won't have him hurt!'

'Won't have him—? You leave me to manage this in my own way, my girl! What in the name of heaven's come over you? I'll speak to you later!'

'Why later? Why not now?'

'What—now?' he exclaimed, almost choking with anger. 'With . . . Nora, do you *want* to be caught?'

'I wouldn't mind,' she answered dully. 'I'm sick of this life—yes, and of you. And if we come through this, I'm going to quit. I don't care what it costs me.'

'Tchar!'

'Oh, you can snort as much as you like. I mean it. I've just about come to the end.'

'Yes, I've heard that sort of prattle before,' he cried savagely. 'And it don't go down with me—not a little bit!' He was by the door, and he now flung it open. 'Now, then, Ben, or whatever you were christened!' he called. 'Come here!'

Ben appeared at the door. His brain was numbed to it all, and he almost bore himself with a swagger. His hands were in his pockets, and he did not close the door, but Brant closed it for him, and turned the key. Then he demanded, bluntly:

'Who are you?'

'Bishop o' London,' replied Ben.

'Don't play the goat,' frowned Brant. 'Why are you here?'

'Lummy, am I here? S'pose I am, but yer can't be sure o' hennythink in this 'ouse, can yer?'

'I say, what are you *doing* here?'

'Oh, doing? That's diff'rent. Collectin' cigarette cards.'

'You'd better be careful!' began Brant, but turned as Henry suddenly reappeared from the passage. 'Well?' he asked anxiously. 'See anything?'

'You can't see your hand before your face,' replied Henry, glancing at Ben, who was strolling jauntily round the room. 'The fog's all round the place. We might be surrounded, and never know it.'

'But didn't you even see the doorstep?' demanded Nora.

'Oh yes, I did get a glimpse of that,' he responded. 'No one. No one at all. Whoever was there has gone.' He jerked his head towards Ben. 'Have you got anything out of him?'

'No, not yet. I'm only just starting,' replied Brant, and

walked across to where Ben was standing. 'Keep still, can't you? You're not on a walking tour! Now, then. What do you know about this murdered man?'

'Oh, lummy,' said Ben with a groan. 'All I knows is that 'is nime was Smith, 'e useter lodge nex' door, and I ain't murdered 'im. 'Corse, I might 'ave done it hin me sleep, yer know,' he added thoughtfully, 'and it might jest 'ave slipped me memory like—'

'Have you any idea who *did* murder him?' interposed Brant.

'Yus, 'corse I 'ave,' answered Ben promptly. 'Gal's father done 'im in.'

'Oh, you think that, do you?'

'Pline as mud, ain't it? One feller's murdered. T'other feller's disappeared. Twice two's four. Clear as honions.'

'Yes, but, damn it, you tell us that *both* have disappeared,' retorted Henry. 'Corpses don't disappear, my man. Are you quite sure you've done nothing with the body?'

'Me? Wot should I 'ave done with it?' demanded Ben indignantly. 'I don't collect 'em!'

'You might have thrown it out of the window,' suggested Brant.

Ben opened his eyes wide.

'Wot for?' he inquired.

'Well, well—if you didn't want the body discovered—'

'Oh, 'corse no one 'd never see it layin' on the pavement, would they?' cried Ben with spirit. 'If I didn't want it discovered! Lor' luvvaduck! Chucked it aht o' the winder, did I? The Merchant Service is gettin' hon!'

Brant swore, and Nora smiled. Henry smiled also, but pursued the point.

'You know, Ben—'

'Bloomin' fermilier, ain't yer, 'Enery?'

'I'm beginning to wonder if you ever saw this runaway corpse at all!'

As he spoke, a shadowy, groping hand slowly rose outside the window. The inmates of the room had their backs to it, and did not see the hand, which groped about for the latch.

''Corse I seed the corpse,' said Ben. 'And 'corse *'e* seed it.' He jerked his thumb towards the inner room. The hand at the window found what it was groping for, and the window began to open. 'That bloke in the next room seed it same as I did. 'E told yer.'

'Yes—who is that chap?' asked Henry.

'Passer-by. When I sees the blinkin' corpse, I 'ops it. I 'ops it outer the blinkin' 'ouse, and blunders inter this blinkin' feller—and then, blast me, 'e mikes me 'op it back agin.'

The hand at the window suddenly shot up, clawed the air, and disappeared. Happily unconscious of events behind him—he had quite enough before him—Ben continued:

'I'll tell yer wot it is. 'E's one o' them narsty conshyenshus fellers wot won't let a thing alone. Carn't close 'is eyes to a narsty sight, like. Know wot I mean?'

'Yes, I know what you mean,' growled Brant. 'Can't keep his nose out of other people's business!'

'That's right. Kind o' bloke they loves in 'Eving, but 'ates dahn 'ere.'

'Yes, yes, I don't want to hear any more comments! . . . Where's that draught coming from? . . . Do you know anything about the diamonds?'

'Diamonds? Me?'

Once more the inmates of the room missed something through lacking eyes in the backs of their heads. The passage door slowly and softly opened, and a figure crouched in the aperture. A big, broad-shouldered figure, with one shoulder higher than the other.

'Now, then, don't pretend you don't know anything about these diamonds,' rasped Brant. 'The telegram mentioned them—'

'Oh, what's the use?' muttered Henry.

The figure at the door, however, appeared immensely interested. While its eyes were alert for any movement that might lead to its discovery, its ears were also alert to miss no word of the conversation.

'The telegram says that the Suffolk necklace has been found,' pursued Brant.

'Well, wot abart it?' demanded Ben. 'Where's yer diamonds?'

'The Suffolk necklace, you fool!'

'Fool yerself!'

'Do you know anything about them? Answer me, or I'll—'

'Oh, yus, o' corse I do,' interposed Ben. 'Look at me guv'nor. I'm orl hover diamonds!' He opened his coat, and thrust out his threadbare waistcoat. ''Ow silly of me. I stole them sparklers larst Thursday week. Or was it Toosday? No—Toosday was the Crahn Jools!'

The figure at the door slipped into the room, and swinging the door wide till it almost met the wall, slid behind it.

'If you think we're here for a joke—!' shouted Brant, raising his hand.

'What's that?' exclaimed Nora.

A scream sounded from the inner chamber. It had barely died down when the room was plunged into darkness.

19

Ben Enters the Cupboard

For several seconds, chaos reigned. Ben instinctively put up his hands, to ward off invisible foes in the darkness; he could see nothing, for the fire had burned low by now, and was nearly out. The other inmates of the room, no less alarmed, stood strained and alert, waiting for the next step without any knowledge of what it would be, or whence it would come. All they knew, for certain, was that a candle had mysteriously gone out on one side, and a shriek had occurred on the other, while a cold draught slithered through a room of which both the doors and the window had been securely closed.

'Oh, Gawd, wot a 'ouse, wot a 'ouse!' chattered Ben's voice.

It awoke the others to action. Brant stumbled to the door of the adjoining room, from which the scream had come, and, as he opened it with trembling hands, a streak of candle-light slanted in. It slanted across to them and beyond them, right on to the door of the cupboard, catching it just as it quietly swung to; but no one saw it swing to, for all eyes were turned towards the light's source.

'Who's in there?' cried Brant, pausing on the threshold.

'Miss Ackroyd got frightened,' answered Fordyce's voice quietly.

'Stay where you are—don't move!' shouted Brant. 'Don't forget, I've got my revolver handy!'

He slipped into the inner room. Henry watched him for an instant, then glanced at Nora.

'Well,' he muttered, 'who did that? Who put out the candle?'

Nora shook her head.

'Not me, guv'nor,' volunteered Ben.

Henry rounded on him suddenly.

'I believe you did, confound you!' he exclaimed.

''Corse I did!' answered Ben, surging on a tide of angry reaction. 'I does heverythink, doesn't I? I kills a man with a lead pencil—'

'Shut up,' said Henry, fumbling with matches, and moving towards the extinguished candle stump.

'—and then I chucks 'im aht o' the winder on a hempty stummick, ter 'ide 'im hon the pavement. Then I blows a candle hover, 'arf acrorst a room.' He emitted a hard, blowing sound, in ironic illustration of his assumed prowess in that direction. 'If I could blow like that, guv'nor, I'd blow the lot o' yer to Jericho! Blarst me, I would!'

With an exclamation of annoyance, Henry re-lit the candle, which had toppled over to the floor, just as Brant returned from the inner room. He closed the door behind him swiftly, and re-locked it.

'Well?' asked Nora.

'Nothing—as far as I can make out,' answered Brant. 'Nerves. The girl got frightened and shrieked.'

'At nothing?'

'So they say . . . Hallo! I said there was a draught! That door's open.' He pointed to the door to the passage. 'It wasn't open before, was it?'

'No,' replied Henry definitely. 'I closed it.'

'When you came up from the next floor just now?'

'Yes.'

'Then how the devil did it get open?'

'Oh, I done it,' observed Ben. 'It's quite heasy. Yer jest stretches aht yer harm and mike it grow, like a telescope—'

'Hold your tongue!' interposed Henry. 'Perhaps it blew open.'

'Yes—look—the window!' exclaimed Brant. 'Wasn't that shut, too?'

'It can't have been,' said Henry.

'Well, we'll have it shut now, anyway,' answered Brant, climbing on to the packing-case beneath it. 'And we'll have it bolted, too.'

'Ah, that won't be no good, guv'nor, not with me abart,' commented Ben. 'I've 'ad a corse at Meskerline and Dervant's, I 'ave.'

'I expect the wind blew in through this window,' suggested Brant, as he fastened it, 'upset the candle, and then blew the door open.'

'Only the door happens to open inwards,' murmured Henry.

'Well, it hasn't blown the fog away,' remarked Nora. 'Can you see anything, Uncle?'

'Not a darn,' he replied, as he sprang down from the case.

'Everything's falling to pieces in this damned house,' said Henry.

'Yus,' replied Ben quickly, to divert attention from his

actions to himself, for under cover of Brant's occupation at the window, he had managed to slip towards the inner door and unlock it. 'The 'ole show'll soon come dahn—and then I hexpeck, yer'll say as 'ow I was the bloomin' hearthquake.'

'Come away from that door!' commanded Brant. 'What have you been up to?'

'Nothink,' lied Ben stoutly.

'I don't trust you, my lad.'

'Queen Anne's dead!'

'And I'm going to put you where you won't be up to any more mischief,' continued Brant, looking around the room.

'Is there sich a plice?' queried Ben innocently.

'Ah, yes—there is,' exclaimed Brant, as his eye lit on the cupboard door. 'We'll put you in there. Here, Henry—give me a hand . . .'

'Righto,' answered Henry, advancing quickly. 'What's the idea? Strap him up?'

''Ere, 'ere!' objected the seaman as they seized him. 'Wot's goin' ter 'appen *nah*?' They did not answer, but, slipping off his belt, began to strap it round his feet. 'Oi! I'll tell the Board o' Trade! Yer surely ain't goin' ter shut me hup in a cupboard—me, wot's stoked a ship the size o' Windser Castle—'

'Brutes!' murmured Nora helplessly.

'Yus, ain't they, miss?' agreed Ben. 'Fust-class brutes! Of horl the hinsults! This is my lucky day, I don't think! Oi—go heasy, there! If yer wants to git hon in the world, find aht the star I was born hunder, and choose another. I'm a murderer. I'm a liar. I'm a 'uman writin'-desk. And nah, blimy, I'm ter be a bloomin' cupboard fitting.'

They lifted him to his feet, and began to carry him to the cupboard.

'There's *one* thing I am yer've none o' yer fahnd out,' exclaimed Ben.

'Oh, and what's that?' asked Brant.

''Ungry,' retorted Ben.

They opened the cupboard door quickly, shoved the unfortunate seaman in, and closed and locked the door. A second's silence ensued. Then, from the depths of the cupboard, rose a muffled roar of terror.

'Huh! Afraid of the dark,' commented Brant, coming away, with a slight shudder.

'You brutes—both of you!' muttered the girl.

Henry, on his way to the passage, regarded her with an odd expression.

'Sorry, but we can't afford to be squeamish in this game, my girl,' he said. 'Unpleasant things have to be done occasionally.'

'Hey—where are you going?' demanded Brant, as Henry resumed his way to the passage.

'I think I'd like another little squint at that front door,' answered Henry. 'If we decide to make a bolt for it, we want to be sure first all's clear, eh?'

He went into the passage quickly, and disappeared down the stairs. Brant gazed after him for an instant, then turned to Nora.

'Wise to let him go?' he queried, looking at her anxiously.

'If you think not,' she replied, 'you'd better go and stop him.'

'That's right! Be funny!'

'I assure you, Uncle, I don't feel at all funny!'

'Nor do I. Now, look here, my girl. This is how I figure

it out. That sailor fellow's a fool—all the same, he hit on the right idea.'

'What idea?' asked Nora dully.

'Why, that the girl's father outed Smith. Ackroyd finds Smith here. Smith had come to keep his appointment here with us, see? That's clear, isn't it? He must have come, because we heard from him—otherwise, *we* wouldn't be here. Very well, then. The two men meet, there's a tussle, and Smith comes off second best. Rum, I admit,' he reflected, 'because Smith's supposed to be a pretty hefty fellow, from all accounts. However, perhaps Ackroyd is, too. Ackroyd—the girl's father—disappears after the tussle. Lord knows where!' He banged his hands together suddenly. 'Yes, that's it, of course. Ackroyd's gone to give the alarm. Ten to one, there's a ring of police round the house at this moment—'

'Yes, that may explain Ackroyd's disappearance,' interposed Nora. 'But it doesn't dispose of Smith's. How do you account for that?'

'I don't account for it. It beats me,' replied Brant distractedly. 'But suppose Smith *wasn't* dead? Suppose he was only shamming—or was only stunned? . . . Look out, Nora! Quick! Behind you!'

The door of the inner room opened abruptly, and a man with a crooked shoulder sprang out.

20

The Man with the Crooked Shoulder

'Good God! Smith!' cried Brant, gasping.

'Yes, Smith,' replied the man sharply. 'Surprised to see me, eh?'

He glanced at Brant searchingly, then transferred his gaze to Nora.

'Where have you been?' asked Brant.

'Not in the next Kingdom, where you expect I've been,' answered the man. 'I've got a tough skin—tougher than yours, I reckon, from the look of you. One needs it for this game. Who the hell's in there with the Ackroyd girl?'

Before Brant could reply, Henry came running back from his tour of investigation.

'Fog's worse than ever,' he said as he entered. 'I rather believe I heard a police whistle. So we'd better—'

He stopped abruptly.

'Hallo! Who's this?' demanded the man, regarding Henry with suspicion.

'It's Smith, Henry—Smith!' cried Brant, delight and relief

in his tone. He seized Henry by the arm, and Henry felt the fingers trembling. 'You see, he's not dead!'

'Smith!' said Henry slowly. 'Why—he—'

'He's been through a tough time, but he's come through all right,' interposed the man. 'I'll tell you all about it later—'

'Yes, but where's Ackroyd?' persisted Henry.

The man smiled ironically. 'Of course, this *is* the time for questions, isn't it? Don't worry about Ackroyd. I've made him safe enough. And if you're all for that ferry train, you'd better hustle. You haven't a great many minutes.'

'Yes,' murmured Henry, still staring at the man, 'we must hurry, of course, but—'

'Did you say you heard a police whistle?' demanded the man.

'Yes—I thought so—'

'Well, that settles it!' barked Brant. 'Come along. He's right—this isn't the time for explanations.'

'No, but we'll be sure of ourselves, just the same,' exclaimed the man suddenly. 'Let's have a look at your tickets.'

Nora held up her badge, and Brant held up his, approaching the man as he did so.

'There—we're square,' he said, and then added, in a quick, low voice, 'I say, Smith, I don't know anything about that other fellow—he's not with us.'

Henry also approached the man, as he took his badge from his pocket and presented it.

'So *you're* Smith, are you?' he frowned.

'Of course I am!' retorted the man. 'The question is, who are *you*? But we can't enter into all that now—'

'There's just one thing we would like to know,' interposed

Nora, and Smith turned and looked at her with an impatient expression. 'Was it really Ackroyd who knocked you on the head?'

'Who else could it have been?' answered the man. 'Of course, if you're set on wasting time—'

'We're not,' said Nora coolly, 'but one likes just a little light, you know—especially before going through a tunnel. How did you disappear from the next room, where you were supposed to be?'

'Don't blame *me* when you're caught,' exclaimed the man angrily. 'If you're really bursting to know—when I came to in the next room I didn't feel quite fit enough to enter into complications all at once. I heard the devil of a noise going on in here, and thought I'd recover a bit before joining in. So I dragged myself into a cupboard—there's quite a useful one—and locked myself in. I didn't want anyone coming along to finish me off.'

'That was quite sensible,' nodded Brant, glancing at his companions.

'Of course it was sensible,' retorted the man. 'Sense is a quality I happen to possess—and to which any number of you folk owe your liberty! When I was fit again, I came out of the cupboard—'

'And made the girl scream,' nodded Brant again.

'Yes—I gave her the scare of her life!'

'But you weren't in the room when I entered it!' exclaimed Brant suddenly.

The man grunted scornfully.

'A lot of infants you are!' he said. 'Didn't I pop back into the cupboard pretty quick when I heard you coming in? You might have been the police! How did I know, in that instant? Anyway, I came out again soon after, and here I am, and if you stop to ask any more questions, it's in gaol you'll be tonight!'

'Yes, yes, you're right,' agreed Brant. 'We oughn't to have—but still, you know—'

'Oh, stop that jibbering,' cried the man, 'and stand by.' He turned back to the inner room, threw the door wide, and called, 'Say, you there! Come in!'

'What's that for?' inquired Henry, feeling for his revolver.

'That's right—and you, too, Brant. Cover them,' said the man. 'We've got to get 'em in here—they mustn't see our little staircase to the tunnel.'

'Oh, it's through there, is it?' exclaimed Brant delightedly. 'Thank God for that.'

'Sh! Here they come!'

Conversation broke off, as Fordyce walked into the room, followed by Rose. The girl was white, but composed. Fordyce himself, whatever he may have felt inside him, betrayed no concern. His attitude suggested that, for the time being, the control of matters was out of his hands—Brant's and Henry's revolvers made that clear—and that the Cause of Respectability he stood for would not be assisted by the gloom. His eyes were watchful, however, and as he glanced round the room he noted the revolvers and the attitudes and position of those who held them.

'Don't be alarmed, Miss Ackroyd,' he said lightly. 'It's only a bad dream. You'll wake up in a jiffy.' She smiled faintly, as he continued: 'The happy family's increased, I see.'

'*Ours* has,' grinned Brant.

'By Jove!' exclaimed Fordyce suddenly, catching his meaning. 'Where's Ben?'

'He's safe enough,' answered Henry, walking towards a case around which was some useful rope.

'Where is he?' repeated Fordyce.

'Minding that cupboard for us, from the inside.'

'I say, Miss Brant,' frowned Fordyce; 'are you a party to this?'

'What can I do?' she asked.

Fordyce looked at her, held her eyes for a moment, and then nodded. 'Yes, that's true,' he said. 'What can you do? It's a pretty stiff current, isn't it?—once one drifts into it.' He turned back to the others. 'I'll promise you this,' he remarked. 'If there's been any dirty work, somebody'll swing for it.'

Henry approached with his rope.

'What's that for?' inquired the man.

'Best truss 'em up,' answered Henry. 'You do the girl, Uncle Brant—'

'That's not necessary,' interposed the man, testily. 'You people seem to love wasting time. We can lock them in here.'

'No; safety first's my motto,' exclaimed Brant, backing Henry up, and taking a portion of the rope from him. 'I'll look after the girl. Tie 'em in chairs; there's another chair in that inner room.' He darted in, and reappeared with a second chair. 'Here, Smith, you do the man, and Henry can stand by with his revolver, for accidents.'

'Well, perhaps you're right,' conceded the man, taking the rope from Henry. 'It will keep them out of mischief for a few minutes—and our business won't take longer.'

Fordyce and Rose were forced into the chairs, and the business of tying them up proceeded rapidly.

'You are a charming crew,' murmured Fordyce. 'It's a pleasure to have met you!'

'But, unfortunately, we can't stop,' smiled the man. 'We're

going to take a little walk—and as there ought to be someone to mind the house, we're leaving you here to do it.'

'I see,' nodded Fordyce. 'So many thieves about, eh?'

Henry approached Fordyce, and examined the rope.

'Can't say that looks like much of a knot,' he commented.

'I've not finished yet, you fool!' snapped the man.

'No. All the same, there's no harm if I help you.'

A minute later, both captives were securely fixed. The man ran to the door to the inner room, cried, 'Everything all right now? Good—then we'll vanish!' and invited the others in.

For an instant Brant hesitated, but Nora ended his hesitation by pushing past him and entering the inner room. Then he followed her, shoving Henry in with him.

But the man did not enter. The moment they were through, he banged the door on them, and swiftly locked it.

'Well done, Ackroyd! Well done!' cried Fordyce.

'Father!' gasped Rose.

'Thank God!' breathed the man, and his voice assumed a softer tone. 'Rose, they haven't hurt you, have they?'

'No, no!' replied Rose, her eyes shining with relief, as a banging started up on the other side of the door. 'Father, you were wonderful!'

'Yes, sir, you're a marvel!' corroborated Fordyce.

'I thought I should never get them out,' said Ackroyd, but his words were almost drowned by the angry cries from the next room. 'Quiet there!' he shouted, and then turned back to Fordyce, to free him from his knots.

'Best bit of bluff I've ever seen, Mr Ackroyd,' remarked Fordyce, 'but we'll hand out the bouquets later. There—I think I can manage the rest, if you'll run and free your daughter now.'

'Yes, yes,' cried Ackroyd. 'I'll get her loose—the damned rascals!'

But Rose shook her head, as he ran towards her.

'No, no, father—Ben first!' she gasped. 'The poor fellow must be suffocating—they said he was in that cupboard. Get Ben out—and then, the police!'

Ackroyd turned, and made for the cupboard. With fumbling fingers—for the strain of the last few minutes had been terrific, and he was now weak from the reaction—he turned the key, while the banging and the angry cries of the trapped trio in the adjoining room grew louder and louder.

'My God!' cried Fordyce suddenly.

For, as the cupboard door opened, a huge form sprang out, and Ackroyd crumpled beneath its weight. The huge form gripped Ackroyd in a gorilla-like clasp, and began to swing him round.

'Hold him, sir, hold him!' shouted Fordyce, struggling frantically to free his feet. 'I'm with you in a second!'

But the huge form was too swift and too strong. In a flash, Ackroyd was swung round and hurled into the cupboard, the cupboard door was slammed and re-locked, and Fordyce found himself looking into the barrel of a revolver held by a fierce and desperate man.

The man had a crooked shoulder—a real one, not a false one. Of greater interest to Fordyce, however, was the fact that, compared with this man, all the other figures in this nightmare appeared mere amateurs at their game. The eyes that glared at him above the revolver had red murder in them.

21

Smith

'One movement,' said the man, in a hissing whisper, 'and you're dead! And so's *she*! Get back into that chair!'

It was clear that the man meant his words, and that he was in a highly excited state that would stop at nothing. But for an instant, even in his extremity, Fordyce hesitated to obey the brutal command.

'Do you hear me?' cried the man fiercely. 'Or is it to be a couple of bullets—right now?'

'Damn you,' muttered Fordyce, as he obeyed.

'And damn you,' retorted the man.

Rose could not speak. She felt suffocated by disappointment and new fear. Keeping his eye on Fordyce, and covering him all the while, the man made his way quickly to the door of the adjoining room, shouting to the angry inmates as he went.

'Stow that row!' he roared. 'Can't you keep quiet for two seconds?'

The voices ceased, but they burst forth again as the door was unlocked, and the prisoners swept back into the room.

'What the—' began Brant.

Even above the renewed babel, the man made his voice heard, and quelled the tide again.

'You durned bone-heads!' he shouted. 'Do what I say, or I'll wash my hands of the whole bunch of you. Don't stand there like sick sheep, but tie that fellow up again while I keep him covered.'

Cowed by his hectoring tone, Brant glanced furtively at Henry. Henry nodded.

'All right, all right,' muttered Brant. 'Don't get so huffy.' He hastened towards Fordyce, grumbling and mumbling as he went. 'It's all very well to shout, but if you'd been through what we've been through—'

'Oh, I've not been through anything, haven't I?' retorted the man, with a jeering laugh. 'Now then—you too!' he cried to Henry, who was following Brant more slowly. 'Get him fixed good and proper. That's not the sort of fellow we can have running about loose.'

'You're right there,' said Brant, as he began to tie Fordyce up again. 'But, I say—where's the other one?'

'What? My double, Ackroyd?' He spoke scornfully. 'So you're growing wise at last, are you? You poor simpletons—infants-in-arms! I've settled with him.' He jerked his head towards the cupboard. 'He's in there.'

Nora shot a quick glance at him.

'You've not—killed him?'

'Maybe,' replied the man callously. 'The damned police spy!'

Rose gave a sob. 'Mr Smith!' she choked.

'Ah—there's someone can vouch for me,' cried Smith. 'The daughter of my precious double. Well, if I have killed him, it mightn't be the first.'

The brutality of his words struck Fordyce like a blow. He could not see Rose from where he sat, but he could guess the agony on her face.

'Your father's safe, Miss Ackroyd,' he exclaimed quickly. 'I can vouch for that. The fellow's only bluffing.'

'Hey—what's that?' shouted Smith, rounding on him angrily.

Fordyce looked at him, white with indignation. 'My God, Smith,' he muttered. 'You are a cur!'

Smith tried to make Fordyce drop his eyes, but could not. The devil rose in him.

'Bluffing, am I?' he menaced. 'Well, you're wrong! *I* don't talk—but this does.'

He thrust his revolver in Fordyce's face, but Brant interposed warningly:

'Steady, steady, Smith. Those things make a row. We don't want a noise.'

Smith hesitated, then lowered the pistol.

'Yes, you're right,' he said with a nod. 'I've got something else in my pocket that will be quieter.'

As he took out the knuckle-duster, Rose gave a little shriek. Fordyce, on the other hand, looked at Smith with unflinching scorn. Possibly Smith only meant to gain the satisfaction of seeing fear dawn on his opponent's face; disappointed in this, his rage rose higher, and he lifted his hand to strike . . .

'Stop that, or I'll shoot!'

The words came swiftly and clearly. Smith's unerring instinct recognised the quality of the tone, and he guessed that something unpleasant was pointing towards the back of his head.

'Nora!' warned Brant.

'I mean it,' repeated Nora. 'I don't stand for murder, Smith.'

'Be careful, be careful!' exclaimed Brant.

'Be quiet, Uncle! He's the one who's got to be careful. Put that back, Smith—or it'll be the last time you'll ever use it.'

Smith's hand had remained suspended. At first he had listened to the sharp voice of the girl behind him with a savage scowl, but gradually a new emotion dawned, and the scowl dissolved. When he turned round slowly, to meet the eyes of his challenger, he was almost smiling.

'So, you don't stand for murder, then, eh?' said Smith.

'No,' returned Nora.

'But you'd shoot *me*?'

'I wouldn't call that murder!'

Smith regarded her with a smile that grew and took on a new quality. He was not in the least afraid, but he was intensely interested. This was quite a new experience for him.

'By God,' he said admiringly. 'You've got some spirit! A bit more than your uncle, eh?' Brant looked sulky. 'Say, you and I would make a fine team, we would.'

'I've no doubt you'd like the chance,' she retorted scornfully.

Smith laughed—a leering, ugly laugh. 'Carry on,' he said, over his shoulder, to the others, and then continued to address Nora. 'I'll tell you this, my beauty,' he said. 'If you shoot me, it won't save your guy there, because I'm the only hope of this little party. If there's an accident to *me*, your friends will soon let *him* know it, eh?'

'That's right,' nodded Brant. 'Don't you be a little fool, Nora.'

'Say,' smiled Smith, 'what'll you give me, my girl, if I treat him pretty?'

'Oh, anything you like,' answered Nora scornfully.

He took an impulsive step towards her, but stopped.

'Good,' he said. 'I'll hold you to that.' He dropped the knuckle-duster back into his pocket, and swung round. 'Got him fixed?'

'Can't budge,' reported Brant.

'Good. Very well then. Now, for the getaway.' Brant began to move towards the inner room, but Smith put his hands on his shoulders abruptly, and turned him round. 'Out in the *passage*, you fool! And down into the basement.'

'Oh,' muttered Brant.

'And hurry, there,' barked Smith. 'We've not got ten minutes before that goods ferry train is due to start.'

Brant hurried out into the passage.

'Ah, we're being led right this time, eh?' he exclaimed nervously.

'Of course we are,' answered Henry, with a glance at Smith. 'Don't you know the real goods when you meet it, Brant?'

'Oh, I'm the real goods, all right,' Smith assured him.

'You bet you are,' said Henry.

'Come on, come on,' cried Brant, turning. 'I'm not going down alone. I don't trust anybody, that's a fact. Here, Smith, suppose you shove along first—and you stick close behind, Henry.'

'Just as you like,' laughed Smith, as though he were humouring children. 'It's all the same to me.'

They trooped out—Smith first, Brant next, and then Henry. Nora, on the point of following, paused and turned towards Fordyce.

'Thanks for saving my life, Miss Brant,' said Fordyce quietly. 'He meant business that time.'

Nora hesitated, then came a step towards him.

'You saved mine,' she answered in a low voice.

'Well, then, that makes us quits, doesn't it? I—I do hope I've saved it to some purpose.' He frowned. 'It's a poor sort of safety you're going to now, you know.'

'Do you think so?'

'I'll tell you something I think. I think you're worthy of a better.'

The footsteps descending the staircase grew fainter.

'The safety of prison walls, for instance?' suggested Nora bitterly.

'Well,' responded Fordyce, 'even that would be preferable, I dare say—if it were the only alternative.'

'It is the only alternative.'

'Don't be too sure,' he retorted cryptically. 'It's a rum world—it never lets you know what it's got up its sleeve. There might be—quite another sort of safety waiting for you. Hang on!'

'What do you mean?' she asked, staring at him.

Fordyce listened. 'I say, Miss Brant—your friends don't seem to have missed you just yet—what about cutting me loose?'

'Yes, yes—I will!' she cried softly. 'Oh, if only I had a knife!' She looked round quickly. 'I know—my file!'

But while she was rummaging in her bag, a hasty step was heard ascending the stairs, and she closed her bag hastily. Murmuring, 'I'll come back later,' she dived into the inner chamber.

'Nora!' called Smith's voice. 'Hey! Aren't you coming!'

As Smith appeared on the landing, Nora reappeared from the next room.

'What's the matter? What happened?' demanded Smith.

'Happened? Nothing,' replied Nora, raising her eyebrows coolly. 'I left my bag in the next room, that's all, and had to fetch it.'

'Oh, that was it, was it?' answered Smith, not attempting to disguise the fact that he did not believe her. 'Well, you've *got* your bag—so now come on!'

He entered the room, and stood by the door while Nora slipped out of it. And he remained standing there for several seconds afterwards, studying Fordyce.

'You think you've done with me, my beauty?' he observed, as he took the key out of the door. 'Well, you haven't. You'll hear from me again.' His eyes roamed round the room, and rested on the empty cases. 'Say,' he remarked maliciously. 'How this place would burn!'

Saying which he laughed, went out, closed the door, and locked it.

22

Through the Window

They listened to his descending footsteps growing fainter and fainter. Suddenly, Fordyce smiled. It was the kind of a smile Mark Tapley might have given in similar circumstances.

'Sweet little fellow, isn't he?' he observed pleasantly.

'He meant to kill you,' answered Rose's terrified voice. 'He'd stop at nothing.'

'I don't know about that,' responded Fordyce, determined at all costs to be cheerful. If his spirit drooped, the girl's would go to pieces. 'He *didn't* kill me, 'cos here I am, all alive-o and smiling! And he *did* stop at Miss Brant's revolver.' He paused. 'She's got some pluck, hasn't she?'

'Yes, she has,' said Rose.

'It was rotten luck Smith coming back when he did,' Fordyce went on. 'In another minute I'd have been free . . . Oh, well, we'll think of some other way.'

Words were easy. But what other way was there? Two people securely bound in chairs, in a room with the door locked against them, have somewhat limited resources.

'Do you think she really means to come back?' asked Rose.

'I'm perfectly certain she'll come back,' responded Fordyce, 'if she gets a chance. But we can't wait for that. Old Smith's got his suspicions aroused—afraid her smart story about having left her bag in the next room didn't quite go down. I say, is there any hope at all of your slipping your knots, Miss Ackroyd?'

She struggled fruitlessly for a few seconds, and then gave up.

'No—I'm afraid not,' she murmured, beginning to cry. 'They're too tight. I—I think—I'm going to faint!'

'No, no, you won't do that!' exclaimed Fordyce briskly. 'Miss Brant's not the only girl I know who's got pluck, eh? Too much grit in your family for fainting. Besides,' he added, 'think of your father! We simply mustn't let him down, you know.'

Rose looked towards the cupboard, and gritted her teeth.

'No, no—I *am* thinking of him,' she said. 'It's all right—I won't faint.'

'Splendid!' cried Fordyce. 'You really are wonderful. You've no notion what a help it is to me to find you sticking it like this.' He strained against his cords, but they refused to yield. He was bound more securely this time. 'Yes, I'm thinking of your father, too,' he went on. To have remained silent would have been a tacit admission of defeat. 'We've simply got to get him out of there, you know—and poor old Ben, too, by George!'

He gazed at the cupboard, and all at once emitted a sharp exclamation.

'What is it?' exclaimed Rose, hopefully catching at any straw.

'Look!' answered Fordyce. 'Smith turned the key when he bundled your father in there—yes, the door's locked right enough—but he didn't shoot the bolt at the bottom. Now, if I could get against that door, with my back to it—I might be able to wangle that key, eh?'

'Oh, can you, can you?' cried Rose, her eyes glowing.

'The policy in this game,' returned Fordyce, 'is to assume that you can do anything. All I've got to do is to discover the chair-step.'

He attempted to move towards the cupboard by a series of jerks. Unfortunately, they moved him farther away from the cupboard, instead of nearer it.

'Doesn't seem to me I've got the chair-step quite right,' he frowned. 'It's a rotten dance, what? Still, there may be some way of doing it.'

'I've got an idea!' exclaimed Rose suddenly, while he considered.

'Well done, House of Ackroyd!' responded Fordyce. 'Let's hear it!'

'Why, you're going the wrong way, aren't you?' she said. 'Well, then, if you could manage to turn your chair round, and did the same thing, you'd be going the right way!'

'By Jove, that *is* a brain-wave!' cried Fordyce, with genuine admiration. 'Upon my soul that's the cleverest thing I've heard for months! And yet it's so simple, isn't it? All really clever things are . . . Of course,' he added, 'when I reach the cupboard, I shall be facing it, with the back of my chair, where my unfortunate hands are, on the wrong side. But I dare say I can swing round again—hallo! Look at this!'

He had half risen, in his effort to turn round, and discovered that he could raise the chair right off the ground while he stood in a stooping position. Then he shuffled back a pace, and sat down on the chair. Repeating the process, he found that he was covering the distance between himself and the cupboard very effectively.

'Ha! I've beaten you, my child!' he declared. 'Your idea was good, but mine's better—though mine, I admit, was an accidental discovery. Now I know what a snail feels like when it's crossing the road with its house on its back! Look, my child—I'm half-way there!'

'Oh, do be careful!' she cried breathlessly. 'If you fell over!'

'I won't,' he assured her. 'That's why I'm taking this little breather, to get my brain steady again for the last lap.'

'Can you hear anything in the cupboard?' she asked.

He shook his head. 'Not a sound. But the door's padded, you know,' he went on quickly. 'I noticed that before—so we wouldn't hear anything, anyhow. Don't you worry, Miss Ackroyd! Your father will come through this all right. He's a wonder. Fancy his keeping the game up all this time—acting for the police, and pretending to be Smith!'

'I suppose it was Smith who stunned him when he came back this afternoon,' said Rose.

'Of course, that's it. And that clears up one mystery. But it doesn't clear up the biggest mystery, does it?'

'What's that?'

'Why, what Smith's game is—and what he's come back for.' He began to operate with the chair once more. 'On with the dance!' he smiled. 'I've changed my opinion of the chair-step. I quite like it!'

As he neared the cupboard, smiling complacently, Rose's eyes suddenly froze. They had strayed towards the window, and she saw a hand feeling about outside.

'Quick—quick!' she gasped.

'I'm being as quick as I can,' answered Fordyce, absorbed

in his occupation, and not noticing the cause of her new alarm; 'but I'm not exactly equipped for speed, you know.'

'There's—there's a hand at the window,' choked Rose.

'What's that?' exclaimed Fordyce, abruptly redoubling his efforts.

'I think it's—it's Smith—come back—'

A head and shoulders, dim and distorted by the fog, now appeared. Rose screamed, and Fordyce felt his forehead become moist.

'Steady, steady,' he muttered. 'It's all right—I've got hold of the key—I've—Good God!'

He had managed to work his fingers over the key, but the position was an almost impossible one. The key lurched out as he gripped it, and slid to the floor.

At the same moment the figure outside, unable to open the fastened window, adopted drastic measures. There was a crash of glass, Rose screamed again, and an arm came through the window, feeling for the latch.

The arm found the latch, and the window was opened wide. Then, out of the yellow fog, leapt a figure.

'Eddie!' shouted Fordyce, almost sick with relief.

'F-Fordyce!' stammered Eddie.' 'M-may I come in?'

Rose's mind reeled, but she managed to retain her senses—just. This new apparition was thoroughly beyond her comprehension—just another of the things that, as Ben put it, simply happened if you stood still and waited for them. But, whatever it meant, one thing was certain. The boyish, smiling youth was not an enemy, but a friend.

'God bless you, Eddie!' cried Fordyce. 'Come here, quickly . . . It's all right, Miss Ackroyd. May I introduce my friend, Eddie Scott? Here, cut these ropes, my lad, and then we'll all shake hands.'

'How do, how do!' jerked Eddie, working like a Trojan. 'W-what's happened?'

'Tell you presently. First, what happened to *you*?'

'M-me? Oh! L-lost you. Chased silly b-blighter coming out of this h-house. M-miles and m-miles. L-lost again. But g-got back. I say, they h-have trussed you up, h-haven't they? F-found your s-silly n-note. P-priceless idiot, you are! R-rang bell!'

'I'll bet that gave 'em a scare!' chuckled Fordyce. 'Go on! What then?'

'No answer,' continued Eddie. 'Rang t-twice. Then tried w-w-water-pipe. Goes-up by w-window here to roof. Got here once. Opened w-window. F-fell down. D-don't kick me—I'll have your l-leg free in a m-minute. F-fell down. Nasty knock. Got a b-big b-bump. But wh-wh-wh-who cares? W-water-pipe again. Perseverance. Thought of B-Bruce's spider. W-wouldn't be beaten by little spider! G-got to window again. Smashed it. And h-here I am!'

'Good man,' cried Fordyce as he sprang free. 'And a splendid story you've told! But mine'll keep, and we'll talk later. Quick, as though the devil were after you. Unlock that cupboard door—key's on the ground—while I—'

He ran across to Rose, and while he unbound her Eddie picked up the key and opened the cupboard door. The next instant he bounded back, as an odd bundle of clothes sprang out at him.

'*Hi!*' exclaimed Eddie. 'What's in here? A j-jack-in-the-box?'

''Oo the 'ell are you?' cried the bundle of clothes, waving its arms wildly.

'Stop, Ben, stop!' shouted Fordyce. 'It's all right, old fellow—you're among friends!'

'Friends?' repeated Ben, gasping, while Rose, now freed also, ran quickly to the cupboard to help her father. 'Fust time 'e told me that'—he laughed wildly to Eddie—''e was sittin' hon me neck, makin' a 'uman writing-desk o' me. Orl friends, 'e ses. Then 'e mikes me turn hout me pockets. More friends! Shouldn't wonder if 'e didn't kiss me in a minute and chuck me aht o' the winder!'

Eddie stared at the strange creature, while Fordyce, torn between desperation and amusement, interposed.

'By Jove, I will chuck you out of the window, if you don't shut up! Where's Mr Ackroyd?'

''Oo's that?' blinked Ben. '*Another* of 'em?'

Fordyce turned, as Rose led her father out of the cupboard. She lowered him gently to a chair. He looked worn out and faint.

'Feeling a bit groggy, sir, I'm afraid,' said Fordyce.

'I'll be all right in a minute,' panted Ackroyd. 'It was that fellow knocked me out.'

'What, Ben?' demanded Fordyce sharply, and turned to the defaulter. 'What on earth—? You are a prize idiot, my lad, if ever there was one. That's Miss Ackroyd's father.'

'Eh? Wot for?' muttered Ben.

'What for? Don't be an idiot!' He took out his flask. 'See if you can keep quiet for just a minute, while I help Mr Ackroyd to recover from the fruits of your idiocy!'

'Jest a minit nothink!' retorted Ben indignantly. 'I've 'ad enuff "jest a minits"! Jest a minit, and some 'un 'its me on the 'ead when I'm shoved in that there cupboard. Jest a minit, and 'e pops aht o' the cupboard. Jest a minit, and 'er father pops hin. Then I gits a bit o' me own back, and fair knocks 'im abart. 'Owcher hexpeck a feller to know 'oo's 'oo, when 'e's in a dark cupboard with blokes poppin' hin and hout that 'e's never seen afore any'ow? Blimy,' he concluded, in a final indignant burst, 'heverybody's 'ittin' *me* abart! Ain't I ter 'it nobody?'

'Oh, I hope to give you something proper to hit presently, Ben,' answered Fordyce, having attended to Ackroyd during this dissertation. 'We've got to catch those rascals yet.'

Ben looked a little blank, while Ackroyd shook his head.

'I'm afraid that's impossible now,' he said. 'We've lost them.'

'Well, *I* ain't hofferin' no reward fer their recovery,' observed Ben. 'If a murderer gits away, I ses, let 'im!'

'Not my view, old son,' smiled Fordyce.

'Nor mine,' agreed Ackroyd. 'All the same, I'm afraid *I'm* finished for the day.'

Fordyce walked to the door, and tried it.

'Don't worry about that, sir,' he said. 'If we can get out of this room, I'm carrying on for you.' He shook the door, but it stood firm. Then he glanced at the window. 'Eddie,' he exclaimed suddenly.

'Yes?' answered Eddie.

'Look here—did you say your water-pipe went up to the roof?'

'Yes.'

'Think you could shinny up it?'

Eddie grinned. 'Rather! That's j-just in my line.'

'Lummy,' murmured Ben. ''E's the cat burglar!'

'Then up you go, my lad,' ordered Fordyce. 'Get on to the roof, and, when you're there, climb across in that direction'—he pointed with his hand—'till you come to a skylight. It's the skylight just outside the door there, so you can easily get your bearings. Drop through the skylight into the passage, and then unlock that blessed door.'

'Reg'ler Napoleon, ain't 'e?' observed Ben.

Eddie was already climbing out.

'B-bet you it won't take me more than sixty s-s-seconds,' he cried.

'It will, if you stop to talk,' retorted Fordyce.

Eddie disappeared, and Fordyce turned back to the others. Rose looked at him anxiously, and he threw her a reassuring smile.

'Work's over for both of you for today,' he exclaimed. 'I'm sure you'll agree, Miss Ackroyd, that your father's done his bit—'

'He has,' she interposed. 'I've made him promise to give this game up!'

'It was an easy promise,' said Ackroyd, half apologetically. 'You see, after this I'm afraid the game will be up, anyhow!'

'Never mind—I expect it's been profitable to the police while it lasted. Your daughter will see you home, and look after you—and also after herself, I hope. She's had a pretty stiff time herself.'

'Yes, I have,' she answered, 'but—'

'No "buts"!'

'I was going to say—*you've* had a stiff time too, Mr Fordyce. Won't you go home too?'

'I couldn't yet,' he replied. 'I owe that brute Smith one. And then—' He paused. 'There's that girl. I'm not very happy about her.'

He glanced up at the ceiling impatiently. They could now hear Eddie creeping gingerly across it. Ben looked a trifle worried. He recalled the last time he had heard that sound. Of course, it was Eddie up there now . . . But—was it 'of course'? Was *anything* 'of course' in this house?

'Bah! Don't worry about that girl,' snorted Ackroyd. 'She's no good—just a dupe of that fellow Brant's.'

'Maybe,' answered Fordyce simply; 'but she saved my life.'

'Did she? Thought you'd be useful to her some day, I expect! No, it's the chap they called "Henry" I'm worried about. It's my belief he's not a crook at all.'

'Who do you think he is, then?' asked Rose.

'I believe he's a detective!'

Fordyce stared at him.

'A detective!' he exclaimed. 'What makes you think that, sir?'

'Well, there's more in this than meets the eye,' answered Ackroyd, frowning. 'I feel sure he was putting up a big bluff—everything he said and did made me think so.'

'I noticed something funny about him too,' interposed Rose, 'when he was searching me, and took the badge out of my pocket.'

'Well?' asked Fordyce.

'He didn't show it to the others. Why didn't he?' Fordyce shook his head. 'He seemed—almost nervous, I thought. Anyway, he *didn't* show it, and *I* haven't got it—'

'There you are!' cried Ackroyd excitedly. 'It was that badge he showed me! I knew he wasn't with Brant and the girl, before Brant told me—I expected those two, of course, but this chap's a mystery!'

'Well, it's one I'll have to try to clear up,' said Fordyce. 'I wish Eddie would hurry—ah, I think I hear him now at the skylight. Did your daughter tell you about the telegram, Mr Ackroyd?'

'Yes.'

'Know anything about it?'

'No. That's another mystery. Never had any dealings with Barton in my life.'

'That's odd.'

'And I don't know anything about the Suffolk necklace, either—barring what came out in the papers, after Sheldrake was caught. He hadn't got the necklace on him, you know—and Barton's sworn to find it. That completes my knowledge of the business.'

'Then why did Barton send you that telegram?' exclaimed Rose blankly.

'I've said, my dear—I don't know,' repeated her father. 'My head's buzzing!'

'Oi!' cried Ben. ''E's dropped inter the passidge.'

'Yes, I hear him,' nodded Fordyce, and went to the door.

'Oi! Look hout!' warned Ben. ''Owjer know it's *'im*?'

'It must be him,' retorted Fordyce.

'Garn—nothin's "must" in this 'ouse,' answered Ben. 'More like it'll be the Shar o' Persher.'

But, for once, the door opened and revealed the expected. Eddie stood in the passage, smiling, triumphant, and slightly breathless.

Rose helped her father from his chair with a sigh of relief. She smiled gratefully at Eddie, and Eddie smiled back, and Fordyce had to speak to him twice to get his attention.

'Here, take this candle, Eddie,' he said. 'You'll need it, while you take them downstairs. Some of the stairs are missing, aren't they, Ben?'

'Yus,' replied Ben, 'and it's time we was too!'

Ben had an uneasy feeling that the time had not yet come, however. While the others were leaving the room, he lingered behind. Something was on his mind, some new angle of the affair. And when, a minute later, Fordyce returned to collect the rearguard of the party, he found Ben in a strange mood.

'Coming, Ben?' he queried.

Ben blinked at him. His eyes were bright, and his breath came rather fast.

'I say—anything up?' queried Fordyce regarding him sharply.

'Eh? No, guv'nor. Nuffin',' answered the seaman. 'On'y—wot's the gime now?'

'My friend Eddie is seeing the others home,' replied Fordyce, 'and after that he is going to find that policeman you used to be so anxious about.'

'Yus. But wot abart hus?'

'Well, I rather thought you might like to come along with me, Ben.'

'Garn! I ain't no good. Yer knows it.'

'On the contrary, the very sight of you cheers my soul!'

Ben frowned, and rubbed his stubbly chin.

'Look 'ere, guv'nor,' he said coaxingly. 'Doncher think—ain't we done enuff—you and me?'

'No, not yet,' responded Fordyce. 'Believe me, old chap, our best work is yet to come.'

Ben continued to rub his stubbly chin. He looked up at the window—yellow an hour ago, but now nearly black. He glanced at the cupboard, in which perhaps he had spent his most uncomfortable time during this most uncomfortable afternoon, and his eyes rested on the cupboard for several seconds, while Fordyce, with considerate patience, kept his eyes on Ben.

What had happened to Ben, in this last minute, to create this new, furtive demeanour?

'Guv'nor,' said Ben. 'Ye'r' lettin' them hothers go 'ome. When are yer goin' ter let *me* go 'ome?'

'What address shall I give the driver, Ben?' queried Fordyce.

'Buckingham Pallice,' responded Ben cheekily.

Fordyce laughed, and clapped him on the back.

'You know, I positively love you, old chap!' he exclaimed. 'Come along, King George!'

'I know yer loves me,' nodded Ben. 'Yer've done nothink but give me yer affeckshun orl the hafternoon. But where are we comin' hon ter now?'

'Well, I vote we investigate the royal cellars. And you can hold the candle this time, if you like.'

'The royal cellars,' murmured Ben as he took the candle mechanically. 'And wot are we goin' ter do when we gits ter the royal cellers?'

'That Ben,' admitted Fordyce, as they began to leave the room, 'is in the lap of the gods—'

'Then 'ere's somethink fer the lap o' the gods!' exclaimed Ben, darting back suddenly to the fireplace, and picking up a bit of broken iron.

'I've an idea, Ben,' went on Fordyce, 'that when we get to those royal cellars, we're going to prove our metal, and I've also a sort of notion that, when we face the real crisis, you're going to prove a pretty useful man.'

'Lummy, guv'nor,' gasped Ben, pausing. 'Ain't we got ter the real crisis yet?'

'Not by a long chalk,' answered Fordyce. 'Now then, get a move on there!'

'Oi!' retorted Ben. 'That ain't the way ter tork to a king!'

23

On the Stairs Again

Once more Gilbert Fordyce and Ben were together on the stairs. By a miracle, they had passed safely through an hour of peril, and had they chosen, they could have descended the stairs, and walked out into the fog, blotting out further danger and joining hands once again with everyday life. But something made Fordyce refuse that foggy sanctuary—and something made Ben refuse it also.

Ben had his moments of wavering, however, on that journey down to the basement, and towards the bottom of the first flight his legs abruptly weakened, and he caught hold of the banisters.

'Guv'nor,' he said.

'Yes, old son?' replied Fordyce.

'Can I sit dahn a minit?'

'Why?'

'Well—I feels sorter faint,' said Ben.

Fordyce looked at him sympathetically.

'Righto—take a breather, if you must. Like a drop of brandy?'

'Does mice like cheese?' replied Ben.

But the grin on the seaman's face vanished as Fordyce felt in his pocket, and gave a grunt of disappointment.

'Damn it,' muttered Fordyce. 'Eddie took it, in case Ackroyd crocked up again.'

'No luck,' observed Ben.

He certainly looked a pathetic object, sitting on the broken stairs. Gazing at him, Fordyce murmured, frowning:

'I wonder if I'm a bit of a brute?'

'Not ezackly, guv'nor,' replied Ben, with a certain degree of magnanimity; 'but yer seems ter fergit I ain't 'ad nothing ter eat orl day.'

'Poor chap!'

'Yus—me larst meal was them pork an' beans—two in the mornin', that was. Terday orter git me fat dahn, swipe me, it ought!'

'Well,' promised Fordyce, 'if we come through this, I'll stand you the best meal you ever had in your life.'

'That'll cost yer a bit, guv'nor,' returned Ben with conviction. 'Sye, guv'nor, yer wouldn't think as I'd sunk a German battleship, would yer?'

'By Jove!' exclaimed Fordyce. 'No, I wouldn't.'

'Well, I 'aven't,' said Ben.

Fordyce laughed. 'You little devil! I shall always love you, Ben.'

'Yus, don't I know it? Yer clings like the hivy!'

'And you ought to appreciate the compliment! Ready to go on again?'

'Yus. In a minit. No good kickin', is it?—'cos, yer see, it's jest come hover me. I was booked fer this 'ere job.'

'What do you mean?'

'Wot I ses. Booked fer it proper. Afore I met you, guv'nor.'

'Oh! How's that?' asked Fordyce.

'Well—there was that badge with "No. 17" on it I come acrost at that inn, when I fust gits inter the bloomin' fog. I told yer—'

'So you did,' nodded Fordyce, looking at him curiously. 'Where was that?'

'Gawd knows! Leyton way, I reckons. Any'ow, I sees the badge, and the bloke wot it belongs ter 'ops off when 'e sees a fice at the winder. Wonder if them two blokes is—' He paused.

'Go on,' encouraged Fordyce.

'In them royal cellars dahnstairs,' said Ben ruminatively.

'What makes you suppose it?' asked Fordyce.

'Well—seems I sorter reckernised that 'Enery feller. A bit like a feller I bumped inter afore I went inter the pub. And if I *was* marked fer this 'ere job, it'd orl work in, like. Yer see, guv'nor, when I 'as a bite o' somethink arterwards, I 'ears two people torkin' low be'ind me, at another table. And, swipe me, guv'nor, if they didn't tork abart this 'ere bloomin' "No. 17" till I gits fair sick of it. And their voices was darned like that gal Nora and 'er blinkin' uncle. "No more 17 fer me," I ses. But I passes this 'ouse—and there's the blinkin' number starin' at me agin. Yus,' he concluded, 'I reckon I was marked hout fer this trip the day I was born, and, blimy, if yer reckoned it hup, I dessay yer'd find I was me mother's seventeenth child!' He added, after a pause, 'And then—on top o' that, I—oh, 'ell!'

He rose gloomily, and Fordyce suddenly laid his hand upon the seaman's shoulder.

'Then you've had enough of "No. 17"—is that it?' he asked.

'Oh, no, guv'nor,' retorted Ben. 'Wot a hidea!'

'Would you like me to release you from it?'

'Wot's that?'

'Look here—you can clear out, if you like.' Ben stared at him unbelievingly. 'I say, you can clear out,' repeated Fordyce. 'In your favourite language, hop it.'

''Op it?' muttered Ben stupidly. 'Wot's the gime now?'

'There isn't any game,' answered Fordyce. 'Only it's just occurred to me that perhaps I really *am* a bit of a brute, after all. I've no right to run you into any more danger—now I know your record's clean.'

''Op it, guv'nor? Yer means it, stright?'

'Of course.'

'Blimy, if that ain't a fair knock-aht,' murmured Ben. 'You lettin' me go like this—after I thort we was glued tergether! And wot'll you do? 'Op it, along o' me?'

'No,' answered Fordyce, smiling. 'I won't hop it. Good-bye, old chap. I've got to move on—'

''Ere—'arf a mo'!' exclaimed Ben, catching hold of Fordyce's arm. 'Why not 'op it, guv'nor—why not? Let's *both* 'op it.' Fordyce shook his head, and tried to detach his arm. 'Why not, I ses,' demanded Ben, refusing to let the arm go.

'Well, I'll tell you why not, Ben,' responded Fordyce gravely. 'Hopping isn't much in my line. We've put one girl into safety, and I won't feel that we've quite finished our job until we've done the same for the other. There—now you've got it.'

'Ah, but the hother's a wrong 'un,' urged Ben.

'Sometimes,' said Fordyce, 'it's just the wrong 'uns who need the greatest help.'

'Yus, I dessay,' mumbled Ben, and suddenly cried, 'Oi! Come back!'

Fordyce had disengaged his arm now, and was hurrying down alone. Gasping, Ben overtook him.

'Look 'ere, guv'nor,' he panted. 'It's goin' ter be a risky job in them royal cellars, ain't it?'

'So risky, Ben,' answered Fordyce grimly, 'that once I get in them, I may never get out of them again. That was why I rather fancied having you with me, to lend a hand.'

'Wot—yer wanted me ter lend a 'and, like?' said Ben, impressed.

'That was the sweet idea. But never you mind now. You cut along—'

''Ere, 'ere,' retorted Ben indignantly. 'Wotcher tike me for? A cahard?'

'Well,' smiled Fordyce, 'I was beginning to give credence to a rumour.'

'I don't know wot that means,' asserted Ben, 'but I ain't *goin'* ter 'op it, see?'

'You're not?' cried Fordyce.

'Not likely,' replied Ben. 'Hinsult.'

Fordyce gripped Ben's hand, and there was real affection in the grip, and in his eye, as he said:

'By Jove, Ben, you're a brick! There's no pluck like the pluck of a man who hasn't got any!'

''Oo 'asn't got any?' demanded Ben with spirit. But a moment later he was clutching Fordyce's sleeve.

'What now?' inquired Fordyce.

'Gawd, guv'nor—wot's that?'

'What's what?'

'There—that big, black thing, comin' dahn the stairs—'

'That's your shadow, Ben,' smiled Fordyce.

'Lor' blimy, so it is,' gasped Ben weakly; and then muttered indignantly, ''Op it!'

24

The 'Royal Cellars'

A train rumbled beneath a room. The room was in pitch darkness, but the sound made by the train—its nearness, its loudness, and its vibration—suggested the room's position, though not, as it happened, its character. It was a basement room.

The train rumbling beneath grew louder, grew fainter, and became a memory in the blackness. A minute ticked by. Then, from somewhere outside, came the sounds of hurried footsteps, and a door swung open.

'In here, eh?' muttered a nervous voice.

'Isn't there any light?' demanded another.

The next instant there was a little click, and the room was bathed in a brilliant electric glow.

The room was a cellar, but it had been converted almost out of recognition. The walls were gay with garish hangings. There were comfortable chairs, a sofa, a serviceable round table, and, in an alcove, a desk. A mat covered the centre of the room, while on the door was a map, and beside it a long list of names.

While the room was obviously a place where business was conducted, its atmosphere was one of comfort—rather luxurious comfort—and bore the mark of individual taste. It was the taste of a man who knew what pleased him, and made no bones about it. Others could be pleased or not, as they wished.

And into this room came Nora, Brant and Henry, ushered somewhat ironically by their host, Smith.

'Hal—lo!' exclaimed Brant, staring around him. 'You do yourself well here, Smith. More like a Chelsea boudoir than a cellar!'

'Very likely,' answered Smith, 'but there's no time to talk. Your train goes in three minutes. Where's that time-table?' He looked towards the desk, but suddenly held up his hand as the clank-clank of trucks sounded below them. 'Hear that?' he said.

'Yes,' replied Brant.

'They're shunting your trucks now. So you can gather time's short.'

He began to walk to the desk, but a question from Henry made him pause. Henry had drawn close to Brant, and, after a nudge, inquired:

'Are you coming with us, Smith?'

'No,' answered Smith bluntly. 'I'm not.'

'Oh! Why?'

'Never you mind about me. I've got several little jobs to settle yet.'

'Yes—but what sort of jobs?' queried Brant.

Smith looked at them impatiently. The devil in him was rarely dormant for long.

'You folks seem to be made up of questions,' he exclaimed. 'What's it to you what I'm staying behind for?

If you want to know, one of my jobs is that unknown quantity upstairs. And the sooner you clear out, the sooner I can deal with that little matter.'

'I see,' nodded Brant. 'How are you going to deal with that little matter?'

'Leave that to me,' retorted Smith, with an ugly expression. 'Ask no questions, and you'll sleep sound.' He laughed unpleasantly. 'There's been a fire in an empty house before now.'

Nora turned to him quickly.

'Smith,' she said, 'I'm relying on your promise.'

'Well,' returned Smith, 'I keep my promises—if you keep yours.'

He looked at her with a meaning she could not fail to understand, and she turned away, to change an unwelcome subject.

'What's that list on the door?' she inquired casually.

'More questions!' said Smith.

'It looks like a Visitors' List.'

'Say a "Departed Guests' List," and you'll be nearer the mark. That's Ackroyd's work.'

'It's an interesting collection of names,' observed Nora, walking towards it.

Smith watched her, impatient, but fascinated.

'Three minutes, I said,' he reminded her.

'Yes, I heard you,' she responded coolly. 'Suppose you spend one of them telling us what you propose to do with us!'

'Right,' answered Smith. 'Stand off that rug, you two!'

Brant and Henry moved off the rug on which they had been standing while whispering together. Bending down and taking up a corner, Smith jerked the rug away, and tossed it aside. Then he moved to the wall by the door, and manipulated a small shutter. The shutter slid aside, revealing a disc and a switch. On the disc were figures and letters. Quickly adjusting them, Smith worked the switch, and a trap-door opened in the spot which the rug had covered.

A big, oblong hole now yawned up blackly at them. Steps led down into it, and smoke issued slowly up out of it. Brant took a step forward, gingerly, and peered down, with a slight shudder.

'Looks like a grave,' he murmured.

'The tunnel's below there,' explained Smith. 'On a siding there's trucks—box trucks—ready for the Continental Ferry train. Two a day. Some of those trucks are supposed to go empty. We'll see that one of 'em doesn't go empty. Got me?'

'Yes,' replied Brant. 'I get you. So that's how it's done, eh?'

'Yes—that's how it's done.'

'Nasty idea,' commented Nora.

'It's been a damned useful idea,' retorted Smith.

'Perhaps—till Ackroyd took it on,' observed Nora. 'Since then it's been rather an awkward idea, I think—judging by that little list on the door.'

'Agreed,' nodded Smith, looking at her. 'Can you think of a better, Nora?'

'*I* can,' interposed Henry, with another glance at Brant.

'I wasn't talking to you,' snapped Smith, and walked to the desk. 'Hell!' he exclaimed, as he took up a time-table. 'I'm wrong—they've changed the time to 5.37.' He shrugged his shoulders, and, walking back to the switch, pulled it, and closed the trap. 'Well, that gives us time for a drink and a biscuit, anyway.'

Henry smiled, and as he spoke in a quiet, smooth voice, Brant suddenly took out his pocket-handkerchief and wiped his forehead.

'Why, that's splendid, Smith,' observed Henry. 'Splendid. I always did hate rushing things, you know.'

'Did you?' queried Smith, on his way to a small cupboard in the wall. His tone suggested that Henry was quite at liberty to talk, if he wanted to, but he must not expect responsible people to listen to him. 'Come over here, Nora, and see my wine-cellar!'

Henry continued to smile. He glanced at Brant, still mopping his brow.

'You see, Brant,' said Henry, 'now we'll have a chance to talk about *my* idea, after all. Sit down, Brant. Plenty of time now. Sit down.'

They sat, one at each end of the table, and Brant eyed Henry anxiously and furtively, bearing an odd resemblance to a dog that has lost its master in a crowd and is not quite sure whether he has found him again. Meanwhile, paying no attention to either of them, Smith opened the cupboard in the wall, and took out a bottle.

'Catch hold of this, Nora,' he exclaimed, appearing to derive pleasure from his use of the girl's Christian name. 'Here's a mouthful of Burgundy that will give your eyes a sparkle.' As she took the bottle from him, watching him closely, he suddenly dropped his voice. 'Listen here,' he said. 'Let those two go. You and I would make a fine team. What do you say?' She did not answer, but continued to watch him. 'Oh, well, the prize is all the better when it doesn't pop straight into your mouth. But I'm going to hold you to your promise, my girl. Remember—I could have knocked the head off that guy of yours upstairs!'

'I'm not forgetting it, Smith,' answered Nora. 'And—I'm not leaving here, just yet.'

Smith smiled. That was enough for the moment. He put

some wine-glasses on a small tray, and held it out to her. She put the wine bottle on it.

'That's right—I'm the waiter this trip,' grinned Smith. 'Come along over to the table there, and I'll serve you with some good stuff.'

He walked towards the table. Henry and Brant watched him approaching. Henry's smile had never left his face.

'Better listen to my idea, Smith,' he said as the grim host reached the table. 'In fact, I'm afraid you'll have to. Don't sit down, and don't lay that tray down—stay just as you are. And, as the photographers say, look pleasant.'

'What's this?' demanded Smith angrily.

'Brant's got his hand in his pocket,' answered Henry, 'and I'm afraid something may go off through it if you move. You see, we rather want your hands occupied with that tray at the moment. If you put the tray down, it's a bullet.'

Smith swore.

'What the hell!' he cried. 'I suppose you think this is one up to you—?'

'Steady, steady—'

'You bonehead! Do you think I'm Ackroyd?'

'Ackroyd?' responded Henry. 'My friend, if we thought that, with that pretty Visitors' List on the wall there, we shouldn't stop to argue. Nearly every fellow on that damned list has been nabbed.'

'Well, I know that! But that's Ackroyd's work. And I'm *not* Ackroyd, so what's your grouch?'

'Yes, yes, we know you're not Ackroyd,' interposed Brant. 'But who *are* you? Who are you when you're not Smith, of No. 17? And why—yes, tell me this—why didn't you give us, and all those fellows on that list there, a hint when you dropped out, and Ackroyd slipped in, to play double-face? Where have you been these last six months?'

'In quod!' growled Smith, wondering what his chances would be if he hurled the tray at Henry and jumped upon Brant.

But Henry was watching him for the slightest movement, and Smith was too old a bird to act rashly on impulse. Impulse had urged him to finish off that fellow upstairs, but wisdom had made him patient. Impulse now urged him to go for these two fools, but again wisdom said, 'Wait. Keep your eyes open. Your chance will come.'

'No monkey-tricks, Smith,' said Henry quietly. 'You see, Brant! He's been in quod for six months. So, of course, he couldn't keep up this game at No. 17, could he? I told you. But what was he put into quod for? Because of No. 17? Oh, no. He was put in quod because a man of his Napoleonic genius always has more than one iron in the fire. And Smith has another name—the name of Mike Sheldrake—'

'You think you're a damned fine orator, don't you?' interrupted Smith savagely. 'But what's all this about, anyway? Suppose I *am* Sheldrake? Very well. What of it?'

'I'll tell you, in a moment, if you'll keep cool,' pursued Henry relentlessly. 'No—don't lower that tray yet. We're dead serious. Aren't we, Brant?'

'You bet,' muttered Brant.

'You were in quod, Mr Sheldrake-Smith, for the theft of the Suffolk necklace, value forty thousand pounds. The necklace they knew you'd stolen, though you'd hidden it by the time you were nabbed.'

'Yes—I hid it all right.'

'You did, all right. So they let you escape last week—'

'What's that?' cried Smith, genuinely astonished. 'They let—? Who let me escape?'

'Why, our dear friend Barton—the fellow who's sworn he'll get that necklace back, or give up the service. One of his little brain-waves. As his men couldn't find the necklace, they decided to let you find it for them. Got it straight now, Smith?'

Smith looked at Henry searchingly.

'Oh—they did—did they?' he answered slowly. 'Well—I *haven't* found it.'

'I think you have,' returned Henry coolly. 'That necklace is in this house.'

'It is? You know a damned lot about it, don't you?'

'You bet I do. I know where to pick up information, Sheldrake, and I know how to hang on a chap that's wanted—'

'Ah!' interposed Nora. She had been listening with thinly veiled contempt on her face. 'That telegram from Barton—"Sheldrake moving." Now I'm beginning to understand. If Barton's after the jewels—'

'Exactly,' cried Smith. 'If Barton's after the jewels, my beauties, there'll be nothing but skilly for any of us!'

Henry laughed. 'Don't you worry,' he observed amusedly. 'Barton never sent that telegram.'

'How do you know?'

'For a quite excellent reason. I sent it myself.'

Astonished eyes were turned on him. Smith remained silent, but Nora and Brant both ejaculated, 'You?'

'Yes, I,' nodded Henry. 'Alone I did it. Of course, we can none of us vie with our dear friend Sheldrake-Smith here—that's not to be expected—but I possess my modest share of Napoleonic qualities. I sent that telegram because, while I was not quite sure of the position here, I wanted to keep that fellow Ackroyd out of the way. I told him to stay where he was—to lie low—'

'Wait a minute,' exclaimed Brant, making no effort to disguise the confusion he was in. He had no Napoleonic qualities. 'You say you weren't quite sure of the position here. Well, how much did you know? Why, if you sent that telegram to Ackroyd, you must have known all about his double-cross here—'

'Yes, yes, but I only tumbled to it last night,' interrupted Henry a little impatiently. 'My simple object was to keep Ackroyd away from here. You'll admit, we didn't want him?'

'No. But he came!'

'Because my wire missed him.'

'I think you might have told us all this before, Henry,' suggested Nora.

'My dear sister,' retorted Henry blandly, 'I had other fish to fry. I'll be quite glad to get out of this unpleasant house, and even of this unpleasant country, but my first object in coming here was to come after Sheldrake—as Sheldrake has come after the diamonds.'

'Oh,' fumed Smith, 'so that was your object, was it?'

'Yes. I'm quite a smart fellow, don't you agree? When the authorities let you escape, you led their 'tecs a devil of a dance through six counties, and you shook 'em all off—but you didn't shake me off. Remember a face at a window, in a little inn Leyton way, that rather disturbed you at lunch yesterday? I was a bit careless then, I admit. But, luckily for me, you thought you were safe in this fog, and so you came along here. So did I. I tracked you last night to this very room—'

'What?'

'Yes, and I hid behind those curtains over there, while you

poked around and cursed to find out what Ackroyd had been doing in your absence. I know that necklace is in this house, Brant, whatever he says, because more than once he went out of this room and began going about the place. But he always came back in a mighty hurry—I expect he'd heard that darned sailor, or it might have been Ackroyd pottering around. Anyway, at last he decided to postpone the hunt—and off he went to wait for a more opportune time.'

'Which was this afternoon,' nodded Brant.

'Exactly. And, of course, I came back too—and, thanks to meeting you and my charming sister on the doorstep, here I am. And—that's my story.'

He turned to Smith, and Brant now whipped his revolver out of his pocket.

'You're beaten, Sheldrake!' cried Brant greedily. 'Don't make a fuss. Trot out the goods.'

'So you're in this too?' demanded Smith, rounding on him.

'Yes. We're all in it. We've come in on the last lap—eh, Henry?—and it's ten thousand pounds apiece, I reckon. Come along, now. Let's have a look at 'em!'

Smith's brain worked furiously. He glanced at Nora, but saw there was no help from that quarter. Brant began to approach him.

'You keep off!' Smith exclaimed fiercely. 'Do you suppose I keep the things on my watch-chain?'

'No, we don't,' responded Henry, rising from his chair. 'But what about your pockets?' He winked at Brant. 'Pull the trigger, Brant, if he moves a muscle.'

'I will, don't you worry,' muttered Brant. 'I'm taking no chances.'

Henry slipped his hand into his pocket, and took out a pair of handcuffs.

'I rather fancy these will come in useful,' he suggested. 'Slip your hands together, Sheldrake, and I'll fix you.'

Smith glared at him, and suddenly gave a shout.

'Handcuffs, eh?' he cried, He swung round to Brant. 'You poor boob!' he roared. 'You were born to be double-crossed, you were! Don't you see, you're being double-crossed again—?'

'Eh?' jerked Brant. 'Now then—'

'Oh, you fool, you fool! . . . Do you want this tray in your face, Henry? . . . Brant, didn't they ever teach you addition—?'

'Stop that!' commanded Henry, advancing quickly.

'Look out for him, Brant,' shouted Smith, backing. 'Cover him, Brant!' Brant paused and wavered. 'Look—he's got out the handcuffs! He's a detective. *He's Barton!*'

And the next instant he hurled the tray in his opponent's face.

25

Into the Tunnel

Smith's aim was good. Before his rival could recover, both Brant and Smith were on him.

'This is damned nonsense!' gasped the overpowered man.

'No, it's not nonsense!' chattered Brant wildly. '*You* keep quiet now, or *you'll* get that bullet! That telegram—why did you sign it Barton?'

'Told you—to keep Ackroyd away!' panted the victim, as he was born down by the superior strength of Smith. 'By God, Sheldrake—'

'Yes, yes, but you knew all about Ackroyd,' cried Brant, now seizing the handcuffs as they dropped from their owner's clutch. 'And the tunnel—'

'Of course he knew,' barked Smith. 'It was his business to know. Don't talk, Brant—slip 'em on him. I've got his hands.' Brant obeyed. 'Yes, "Henry," and *you've* done with talking for a while, too,' added Smith with a savage grin.

'I tell you, Brant, you're making a mistake—'

'Yes, I made a mistake when I trusted you!' retorted Brant.

'You did,' said Smith, as he gagged the unfortunate man.

'You might have known he was a 'tec, sneaking in here after me last night . . . There, now his mouth's closed. And, as he's so fond of that little spot behind the curtain there, he can go back to it. Here, hobble his feet first with the strap off that bag, Brant. You see, we've got every convenience here! Quick, now—you've not forgotten you've a train to catch.'

'Haven't we any decent feeling left?' murmured Nora, who had stood apart, a silent, tragically contemptuous witness.

'Don't listen to her, Smith,' exclaimed Brant. 'Here's the strap . . . Damn it all, she can't expect us to be gentle with a detective—and Barton, of all people.' They carried him to the curtain, and deposited him behind it. 'There—that settles him. When's that train go, Smith?'

Smith consulted his watch. 'Another six minutes,' he said, turning to Nora.

'God! We're in a tight corner,' muttered Brant. 'We've got to make a dash for it, and no mistake.'

'Yes, we'd be a nice little haul for the police, wouldn't we? What do they want you for, Nora?'

'Oh, what does it matter?' exclaimed Nora.

'Post-office robbery,' said Brant not sorry to be informative. It was pleasant to recall that he had got the better of somebody.

'Post-office robbery!' laughed Smith. 'I'll teach you a bigger game than that, Nora!' He asked Brant, 'Get much?'

'That's my affair,' retorted Brant.

'As you like,' answered Smith, shrugging his shoulders. 'And I reckon this train's your affair too. So—'

'Yes, yes, but wait a moment,' interposed Brant anxiously. 'I—that is—well look here, Smith—what about that necklace?'

'That's my affair,' said Smith.

'Oh, yes, of course, but—'

'You don't really suppose the diamonds are here, do you?' cried Smith suddenly. 'I don't believe that's a head you've got at all, Brant—it's a bit of soap! My job's to put people off the scent, not on it. And your train's due. Going on it?'

The two men looked at each other. Brant, alone, was helpless, and he knew he was helpless. Well, well—better accept the situation. 'But damn him,' he thought. 'Those big fellows have all the luck!'

'Going on it?' repeated Smith.

'All right, all right,' snapped Brant. 'Don't get huffy. Open your gate!'

Brant's hand had gone into his pocket. Smith smiled amusedly.

'So we don't trust each other even yet, do we?' he observed.

'Oh, get on with it, do!'

'Yes—if you'll go over to that wall first.'

'What's wrong with the level?' queried Brant.

Side by side, they walked to the wall with the shutter. Smith laughed, as he began to work the mechanism. Brant watched him with interest.

'What's the magic word, eh?' he inquired.

'Look, and you'll see,' answered Smith.

'Clever bit of mechanism,' said Brant. 'Does it work from outside too?'

'Yes—both the trap and the door—when you know the combination.'

As he spoke, the trap in the floor opened, and Brant turned towards it with a little shiver. He glanced at Smith again, then jerked his head towards Nora.

'God, it's the hell of a hole,' he muttered. 'You go first, Nora.'

'I'm not going with you, Uncle,' answered Nora quietly.

'What?' exclaimed Brant. 'Not going with me?'

'No.'

Brant threw up his hands in despair, as he heard the colliding of trucks from below.

'What's happened to everybody today?' he demanded. 'Stop this fooling! We've got to look lively.'

'Yes,' nodded Smith, with a queer smile. 'Those who *are* going had better hurry. Listen—when those trucks stop banging . . .' He paused. Then, when all was silent down the smoking hole, he said sharply, 'Now's your chance, Brant. Miss this, and you may have to wait another day—and quite a lot can happen in twelve hours.'

'Nora,' coaxed Brant, 'come on. You'll be caught like a rat in a trap, if you stay here.'

'I've quite made up my mind,' she replied.

'But what's the reason?'

'When I told you I'd finished with you, Uncle, you didn't think I meant it. But I did mean it. We may as well say good-bye inside this room as anywhere else.'

'You've been putting her up to this, Smith,' challenged Brant.

'She is free to do as she likes,' responded Smith. 'Do you really want to stay, Nora?'

'Yes,' answered Nora faintly, after a short pause.

'Good. You shall,' remarked Smith. 'Two to one again, Brant. You can never get the odds, can you?'

In impotent exasperation, Brant strode to the trap-door. He looked down into the unsavoury hole, and at the steep, ladder-like steps that descended into it. Then, suddenly, he began to climb down. Just before he vanished he raised his head and shouted, 'To hell with you both!' Smith laughed jeeringly back.

Brant was gone. Now, apart from the gagged man behind the curtain, Smith and Nora were alone. She looked at him apprehensively as he kicked the broken bottle and glasses into a corner, and produced a fresh bottle from the cupboard. He walked leisurely, thoroughly enjoying the position, and his mastery of it. Placing the fresh bottle on the table, and still without a word, he returned to the cupboard for glasses. These too he placed on the table, smiling to himself all the time, and watching the girl out of the corner of his eye.

Then, with a grunt of satisfaction, he approached her.

'Keep off!' she cried sharply.

'I reckon I've kept off long enough,' he retorted.

'Yes, but wait! Don't misunderstand me!'

'Misunderstand you?' He laughed. 'Oh no! I don't misunderstand you.'

'Keep off—keep off, I say,' she repeated, backing as he continued to approach. 'Do you hear?'

'Well, I was born with two ears,' he replied. 'You've got some spirit in you, haven't you? Well, I like a girl with spirit. I've wanted one for six months.'

'And maybe you'll have to want a little longer yet,' she shot back at him. 'We've not settled our terms yet, you know.'

Smith's brows darkened slightly.

'Now then—don't be a little fool!' he said. 'You didn't expect I was going to wrap you up in cotton-wool, did you? Or—have you some other game on? Aren't you accepting my offer?'

Nora hesitated. 'Yes—but on terms,' she answered, in a low voice.

'Terms!' repeated Smith contemptuously. 'What terms?'

'Keep your distance, and I'll tell you.'

He looked at her, and then at the table with its pleasant invitation.

'Oh, well, why not?' he exclaimed, going to the table. 'Our time's our own. Those fools upstairs can wait till they rot, for all I care.'

'Yes, it's—it's about them I want to speak,' said Nora.

'Well, go ahead. Only have a drink first.' He poured out a glass, and held it towards her. She shook her head. 'Stubborn, eh? Oh, well, just as you like.' He drained the glass, and smacked his lips. 'That's better than the stuff they've been giving me lately. Fire away, my girl. What are these terms of yours?'

She faced him squarely.

'My terms are these, Smith,' she said, 'and no less. You don't hurt a hair on the head of anyone in this house. You let me go up and set free those people upstairs—they won't hurt me—and you unbind that detective behind the curtain, and put him outside this room.'

Smith regarded her admiringly.

'Quite an ultimatum!' he pronounced. 'Very pretty! And what do *we* do? You and me?'

'Oh—anything you like!' she responded. 'The Continent—anywhere we can get. But we start at once.'

Smith drained a second glass, and rose.

'Yes, by God, we'll start at once!' he cried, while the wine flowed pleasantly through him. 'And we'll make a fine team? That's the idea, Nora—clear out of the country—break new ground!' He paused suddenly, and looked at her thoughtfully, unpleasantly. 'Yes, but many a poor bird has been winged on its way to the Continent. That's all in the future! Look here,' he went on, drawing closer, 'if I agree to your terms, as you call them, what do I get—now? *Now?*'

'Now?' murmured Nora, drawing back.

'Yes, now!' He stretched forward abruptly, and caught hold of her arm. 'Nora, give me a kiss!'

'No—I won't!' she answered, her voice trembling.

'Won't? I tell you, if you don't you know what'll happen to that guy of yours upstairs. Oh, don't look so high and mighty! Do you think I've not got eyes, and a brain? Do you think I care a damn about those others—or about that fellow behind the curtain there? Come, give me a kiss. One can only dream of kisses in prison!'

He tried to draw her towards him, but she pushed him away.

'No, no—your part of the bargain first!' she gasped tumultuously.

He seized her again, more firmly.

'Oh, you beauty!' he exclaimed. 'I don't need to make terms with you—I can get all I want for nothing!'

'You beast, you beast!' she sobbed.

He kissed her passionately, then let her go suddenly.

'Beast, am I?' he cried. 'No, wait a minute. I'll show you—I'll show you, Nora! What would you say if I were to put a diamond necklace round that pretty throat of yours? A diamond necklace, my girl, worth forty thousand pounds? Ah, that'll make you change your tune—that'll buy your kisses! Look, Nora—look—!'

He put his hand into his pocket, and as he did so, a change spread over his face. A new passion enveloped it—an agony of amazement and wrathful disappointment. For a few seconds he stared at Nora, dazed, while she, dishevelled, stared back at him. Then, in a hoarse whisper, he gasped:

'Gone!'

The word awoke him to action. With an oath, he rushed to the wall and worked the lever with trembling hands. Slowly the door to the dark passage swung open, and, as it did so, two figures leapt into the room.

'On him, Ben!' cried one.

'Git 'is legs!' yelled the other.

Nora fell back with a sob, and clasped her hands. The figures swung and swayed around the room. Then, in a lightning flash, the smallest hit the biggest with a piece of broken iron, the stricken man clutched the air, toppled—and fell down the yawning hole into the smoky blackness.

26

The Necklace Turns Up

Fordyce, recovering from a nasty blow, found Nora bending over him. For the moment she was all he saw, and the relief in her eyes was no greater than the relief in his.

As soon as Smith had fallen down into the tunnel she had run to the wall and closed the trap-door, following a blind impulse to place one further barrier between her and the terror Smith had stood for. Her distraught condition was reflected by this action, since Smith was obviously in no condition to do her any more harm. Then she had closed the door.

Now, as Fordyce looked up at her, her mind swung to happier but still anxious thoughts.

'Are you badly hurt?' she asked.

'No, I don't think so,' replied Fordyce. 'We managed to get loose upstairs—tell you about that later—whew! that chap winded me!'

'Don't talk, if—'

'Oh, I'm all right . . . Then we got outside that door there, and were wondering how on earth to get in when it kindly opened, all of its little self. The way that relic of the Merchant Service jumped on Smith! . . . By the way, where *is* Ben?'

''Ere,' replied Ben, from the floor.

Fordyce turned and stared at him.

'What on earth are you supposed to be doing?' he inquired.

'Sitting on the plice where 'e went dahn, in case 'e pops hup agin,' answered Ben.

'Small fear of that, old son,' remarked Fordyce gravely.

'P'r'aps, but I ain't takin' no charnces,' retorted the sailor. 'And, wot's more, I ain't messin' hup me pocket-'ankerchiff fer 'im.' He chuckled. 'Best bit o' manslaughter, guv'nor, I hever seed!'

'I second that,' nodded Fordyce. 'Didn't I say you'd come up to scratch when the moment arrived?'

'Yus. Ye'r' always right, guv'nor, if yer waits long enuff. Yer've been tryin' ter mike me hout a murderer orl the hafternoon, and now, blimy, yer've done it!'

'Well, don't worry, old chap,' smiled Fordyce. 'You won't be hanged for it. Hallo!' he exclaimed. 'Who closed that door?'

'I—I'm afraid I did,' answered Nora.

'Oh! Any special reason, Miss Brant?'

She shook her head a little dazedly. 'No. I don't really know. I just pushed it to—after closing the trap—'

'Quite right, miss,' interposed Ben. 'Keep the spooks hout. I'd 'a' done the sime meself in a minit.'

'H'm,' murmured Fordyce. 'It's one of those secret trick doors, isn't it?'

'Yes. I think so,' answered Nora.

'Know how to open it?'

She shook her head again. 'I'm afraid I don't.'

'Well, what about the trap-door? Do you know how to open that?'

'No.'

'Lummy!' gasped Ben shakily. 'Are we locked in, guv'nor?'

'Looks rather like it, old son,' replied Fordyce, and, rising, walked across to examine the complicated mechanism. 'I expect it works by some secret combination,' he said.

They watched him, while he tried unsuccessfully to discover the solution.

'P'r'aps I could do it, guv'nor?' suggested Ben. 'A sailor knows abart knots.'

'Go ahead, then,' answered Fordyce, and turned to Nora. 'Thank the Lord, you're safe, anyway, Miss Brant.'

'Why do you say that?' she asked.

'Why shouldn't I?' he retorted. 'I say, that wine looks rather good! Would you like a glass?'

'No, thank you. But perhaps you would?'

'I would,' he admitted, and she ran to the table to pour it out for him.

'Wot's that—wine?' exclaimed Ben, coming away from the wall. But then he hesitated. 'No, better not, guv'nor—not on a hempty stummick. 'Unk o' bread 'd be more in my line.'

'Well, I'll give you a whole baker's shop one day,' responded Fordyce.

'That'll be in 'Eving,' muttered Ben, 'if we don't find the way hout o' this blinkin' room. I'll never go in a room agin, I won't. As soon as yer gits in, they *claws* yer, and it tikes yer hours ter git hout agin. I—' Suddenly he leapt in the air. He had been walking by the curtain, and had put his hand against it. 'Oi! Oi!' he shouted.

'What is it now?' exclaimed Fordyce.

'Corpse!' reported Ben sepulchrally. 'Another of 'em!'

'Good Lord—'

'My Gawd, guv'nor,' said Ben seriously, 'someone *sows* 'em in this 'ouse, and they comes hup like buttercups and daisies!'

'He's a detective,' interposed Nora quickly, and Fordyce paused abruptly on his way to the curtain. 'He's not dead. They bound him.'

'Detective, eh?' frowned Fordyce.

'Yes,' she nodded. 'Please release him. They fixed him with his own handcuffs. Look—there's the key on the table.'

Fordyce picked up the key, but still he hesitated.

'I suppose it's the fellow who was with you—the one called Henry?' he queried.

'Yes. But that was only a pose. He was found out, and they tied him up.'

'But, surely,' said Fordyce, 'you don't want me to release a detective?'

'Yes—of course.'

'Before you've had a chance to slip away?' She nodded. 'You know what that'll mean to you?'

'Yes. But I'm cornered anyway, aren't I?'

'Not if you make your dash for freedom first?'

'Freedom!' She spoke the word bitterly. 'You were right. There's no freedom for my sort.'

He shook his head gently.

'No, I didn't say quite that, if you'll remember, Miss Brant.'

'Oi,' whispered Ben.

'One moment, Ben. Look here, Miss Brant, I haven't quite got the hang of this yet. Where's your uncle?'

'He's gone,' she told him.

'Why didn't you go with him?'

'I preferred to stay behind.'

'Yes, but *why*?' he insisted.

'Oh—does it matter?' she asked.

'I'm beginning to think, Miss Brant, it matters very much,' murmured Fordyce.

'Oi! 'Ow much longer are yer goin' ter stand there jawin', while this 'ere bloke sufferkates! Don't *that* matter?' demanded Ben.

'Right!' sighed Fordyce. 'Carry on, my rough diamond.'

'Wot's that—di'mond?' exclaimed Ben, starting.

'I said, carry on—and let's hope we're assisting in the cause of humanity!'

'You'd hassist in any cause,' mumbled Ben. 'Yer was marked fer it!'

They pulled the curtain aside, and quickly unbound and ungagged the gasping man. He was not seriously hurt, but he took several minutes to recover. The wine assisted him. When he was in a fit condition to speak, Fordyce asked:

'Feeling better?'

'Yes, thanks,' he nodded.

'They tied you up properly, didn't they? What happened?'

'They got wise to me—found out who I was . . . Yes, I should like another drop, please . . . They did me in, just as I thought I'd got my net over them.'

'Who are you?' asked Fordyce.

'I don't suppose there's any harm in telling you now,' he replied. 'I'm police department.'

'Good Lord!'

'As a matter of fact—I happen to be Barton.'

Fordyce whistled.

'I say! You're not really—Barton himself?' he exclaimed, with a glance at Nora.

'Yes, himself. I've been tracking Sheldrake and the Suffolk diamonds ever since we let the rascal break prison.' He frowned. 'And now he's—'

'Dahn the well, guv'nor,' interposed Ben. 'Dahn the well, with a crack on 'is cokernut!'

'Poor devil! Brant had better luck. He got away. But I don't expect he'll get far. I've got my men posted. And, meanwhile, I see, we've got the girl.'

'Yes, you've got me, Mr Barton,' she answered quietly.

'But perhaps the law might be lenient in her case, eh?' suggested Fordyce. 'She needn't have stayed behind, inspector!'

'No, she needn't, but she did,' he responded dryly. 'And, as a matter of fact, sir, I happen to guess pretty shrewdly *why* she stayed behind.'

'Really,' said Fordyce. 'Why?'

'Perhaps you'd like to tell us, Miss Brant.' Nora was silent. 'Come, why was it?'

'If—if you really want to know,' she answered, 'I stayed behind because I—I mistrusted Sheldrake.'

'Interesting. In what way did you mistrust him?'

'I thought he might be up to some fresh game, dangerous to you—and to Mr Fordyce.'

'The pose of virtue hardly suits you, Miss Brant,' came the icy response. 'How did you propose to stop this fresh game, as you call it?'

Nora bit her lip. 'Oh, I don't mind what you think,' she muttered. 'You can think what you like.'

Fordyce approached her. 'Please,' he said quietly. 'We'd like to hear.'

'Very well, then,' she answered, turning to him. 'I offered to become Sheldrake's—working partner, if he'd undertake to let you get safely away.'

Fordyce regarded her fixedly for a moment. 'I call that rather sporting.' An ironic laugh swung him round. 'You know, she doesn't sound at all like a crook to me, inspector!'

'That's because you haven't my experience of crooks,' he retorted. 'You don't understand their tricks, as I do.'

'I dare say not,' murmured Fordyce. 'But I've a theory that some of the crooks are crooks by nature, and others by circumstance.'

'All the same, believe me. Why, that was a typical crook story. Sob stuff. Just moonshine!'

'Yes, but look here,' exclaimed Fordyce testily. 'What other reason *could* she have had? Let's hear *your* suggestion. I may not know much about crooks, but I know enough about police to know that they always have a theory—and it's nearly always the wrong one. Now then, inspector, trot out your suggestion!'

'I suggest to you, Miss Brant,' he said, turning to the girl, 'that you stayed behind because you knew that Sheldrake was certain not to be far from the diamond necklace formerly worn by the Duchess of Suffolk.'

'Eh? Wot's that?' jerked Ben suddenly. Despite his resolution, he had fallen to the temptation of the wine, and was just finishing his second glass.

'The suggestion is not true, Mr Barton,' replied Nora.

'Nevertheless, I still suggest it,' he returned, regarding her searchingly. 'I suggest that it was quite worth while making up to Sheldrake, Miss Brant. And I will go even further, and suggest that Sheldrake actually showed you the necklace here, in this very room, and placed it round your neck?'

'Wot's that?' exclaimed Ben, his eyes popping.

'That's not true, either,' said Nora quietly.

'I'm sorry, but I have the evidence of my own ears—'

'I tell you, it's not true, Mr Barton,' she repeated. 'If I had the necklace here, I'd give it to you.'

''Ear, 'ear,' nodded Ben vigorously. ''Ere's 'ow!'

'Steady, Ben,' murmured Fordyce warningly. 'Inspector, I feel sure Miss Brant is telling the truth—'

'Unfortunately, I don't share that view,' he interposed, 'and, in the present circumstances, *my* views go. I'm afraid we'll have to search you, Miss Brant, if you've no objection?'

'I have—a very strong objection,' answered Nora.

Fordyce's frown deepened.

'I say—look here,' he exclaimed. 'Don't let's be too hasty over this, inspector.'

'I don't want to seem rude,' came the sharp response, 'but aren't you rather exceeding your rights? Kindly let me handle this in my own way!'

'Well, I don't want to seem rude, either,' responded Fordyce, 'but if your way means any unpleasantness to Miss Brant—well, I'm damned if I will!'

The official voice controlled itself with difficulty.

'I wonder if you realise—Mr Fordyce?—that you're on rather delicate ground yourself, and that, from an official point of view, your interference is unwarrantable. There is such an offence, you know, as interference with the police in the performance of *their* duty. Of course, if you persist in wilfully misunderstanding me—'

'No, inspector, I'm not wilfully misunderstanding you,' interrupted Fordyce, 'but I'm just trying to give a girl a fair chance, and the whole of Scotland Yard wouldn't convince me that I'm wrong.' He turned to Nora. 'Miss Brant—you say you haven't got the necklace?'

'I'll swear it, if you like.'

'No, your word's good enough for me. Do you know anything about it?'

'Yes, but very little more than Mr Barton knows himself. Sheldrake came back to this house to get the necklace—I've learned that—and I believe he did get it, because he *offered* to put it round my neck. But when he felt in his pocket, it was gone. He'd lost it—yes, it's true, Mr Barton,' she insisted, as he made an impatient gesture. 'He was rushing out of the room when—'

'Well, what do you think of that?' he interposed. 'Quite the thinnest story I've ever heard, Miss Brant! I actually heard Sheldrake say he would put the necklace on you, while I was behind that curtain.'

'If you heard that, Mr Barton, then you must also have heard the terms I made with Sheldrake—yet you're trying to make out that my one thought was the necklace.'

'Bah! I knew what was behind those terms. Come along. I'm going to search you!'

He advanced towards her, and suddenly found Fordyce in between. Fordyce's fists were clenched, and they looked quite useful fists.

'Sorry it's got to come to this, Mr Barton,' murmured Fordyce.

'Well, it hasn't—quite,' returned the other fiercely. 'And at least you'll admit, Mr Fordyce, that I'm doing all I can, and exercising a good deal of self-control, to prevent it! Perhaps the police will accept your testimony as to the prisoner's spotless character,' he added dryly, as he walked away towards the desk in the alcove. 'I'll make a note of that in my report. Miss Brant, you've got a couple of minutes still. Produce the necklace before I've finished my notes, and I give you my word you can go free.'

Saying which, he sat down at the desk, his back to them, and began to write.

Nora looked at Fordyce helplessly, flushed, and lowered her head. Then Fordyce, watching her, felt a gentle tug at his sleeve. Ben, with a queer look in his eyes, was trying to attract his attention.

'Think 'e means it, guv'nor?' queried the sailor unsteadily.

'Well, he said so,' replied Fordyce.

'Wot—let 'er go, if them sparklers turns hup?'

'That was his observation.'

Ben passed his hand across his forehead. 'Is this room goin' rahnd?' he asked.

'No, it's quite stationary,' smiled Fordyce. 'I expect it's that Burgundy on an empty stomach, old son.' He paused, but as Ben's mind seemed to be going round as well as the room, he turned back to Nora. 'Don't be down-hearted, Miss Brant,' he said. 'Detectives aren't trustful, you know—it's their business not to be.'

'Oh, I don't blame him,' she returned, in a low voice. 'Why should he believe me? Why—do you?'

He reflected a moment.

'Well, I'll tell you,' he said. 'I believe you because I believe in instinct even more than in logic. And instinct, after all, is simply the deeper logic we can't explain. I trusted you the moment I saw you. And, by the way—here's a little surprise for you. Today isn't the first time I've seen you.'

'I don't understand,' she replied, puzzled.

'Ah, the greatest things in life are those we understand the least, Miss Brant. For instance, do you understand why you refused to make your dash for liberty?'

'I told you.'

'You gave me the words. But can you explain the impulse? There you are! And here's another thing. Can you explain why you and I are chatting together like old friends while your liberty's ticking away in that corner over there?'

She looked at him quickly, and her flush deepened.

'Do you really feel as though we were old friends?' she asked.

'By Jove, I do,' he replied. 'And I've got an idea we're going to be better friends. I say, Miss Brant—look here.' He took his case out of his pocket, and scribbled something on a piece of paper. 'I've got rather a decent old aunt. She lives in Normandy. She's perfectly sane, excepting in two particulars—she hates the conventions, and she's rather fond of me.' He handed her the paper. 'There's her address. If you win through to the Continent—no, *when* you win through to the Continent—don't let's be pessimistic!—look her up.' She stared at him. 'She'll expect you. I've rather a funny habit of looking ahead.'

'But—why are you doing all this for me?' she exclaimed, her eyes filling with tears. 'Do you know what I am?'

'Rather! That's why. Oh, hang it all, Miss Brant, thousands of people go wrong just because Fate's never given them a sporting chance . . . Yes, yes, what is it, Ben?'

The sailor had approached again, and was once more tugging his sleeve.

'Got an idea, guv'nor,' whispered Ben.

'Out with it!'

''Is back's turned. Splice 'im up agin!'

Fordyce smiled broadly.

'What on earth for?' he demanded.

'Blimy, guv'nor,' muttered Ben, 'I can't mike yer hout! Time's nearly hup, ye'r' sweet on the gal—'

'Hey!'

'—and it's 'er larst charnce! Splice 'im up agin, and 'op it!'

'You know, you really *are* a charming idiot,' replied Fordyce, and even Nora smiled at Ben's crestfallen face. 'The verb to hop seems to be the only one you know. And how on earth do you propose to hop it, with all these closed doors? Besides, Ben, there's a little mirror on the wall, over the desk where our friend is sitting, and he's watching every movement. Even detectives aren't complete asses, you know!'

'Looking-glass, eh?' muttered Ben. 'Lummy, I never thort o' that.'

'Cheer up! You've done your bit, anyway, as I knew you would. Your sheet's clean.'

'Done my bit, 'ave I?' murmured Ben.

'Of course you have!'

Ben shook his head gloomily. 'Blarst yer, yer'd draw the 'eart out of a gum-drop!' He turned and walked towards the desk. ''Ere, detective—!'

The man at the desk swung round. His eyes had been on the little mirror more than on his paper.

'Well, what is it?' he demanded.

'This,' said Ben; and, diving into his pocket, produced a case. ''Ere's yer bloomin' sparklers—and Gawd bless yer, I don't think!'

27

Final Surprises

Almost before the words were out of Ben's mouth, the case was seized from his hand. He had certainly electrified his hearers, and through the confusion of his emotions—a confusion both psychological and wineful—there ran pleasure and pain. It was pleasant to feel that he, in this house of surprises, had sprung a surprise himself, and it was painful to find himself relieved so instantaneously of the richest burden his pocket had ever borne.

''Ere, don't snatch!' he complained indignantly. 'It ain't nothink ter eat.'

'How the—!'

'And don't chip in while I'm a-torkin',' continued Ben. He jerked his head towards Nora. 'She 'ad them sparklers, detective, as yer sed. Give 'em ter me, she did, ter give ter you. So now ye'r' goin' ter let 'er orf, ain't yer?'

'My God, yes!' came the excited answer. 'If the necklace is really inside.'

'Oh, the sparklers are there orl right, Mr Fumble-Fingers! There, wot did I say?' he went on, as the fumbling fingers operated the catch, and the lid came open, revealing flashing hues beneath.

'Bit of orl right, ain't they?'

'But, Ben,' exclaimed Fordyce, 'I didn't see Miss Brant give the case to you!'

Ben winked hard. 'Didn't yer?' he said innocently.

'No. And Detective Barton seems to have missed it in his little mirror too—'

'I *didn't* give it to him,' interposed Nora, disregarding Ben's further winks. 'He's just doing it to help me—'

'Oh, orl right!' grumbled Ben, giving it up. 'Seems as 'ow I carn't do nothink like I wants ter! 'Ave it yer own way. She never 'ad 'em. There. No—*I* 'ad 'em!'

'You, Ben?' cried Fordyce.

'Yus—took 'em orf that Sheldrake bloke when 'e and me was in that there cupboard hupstairs. Nah, then, keep quiet fer the Merchant Service, fer once in yer lives, and I'll tell yer.' He looked round at the company, and found all the silent attention he required. 'Yer see,' he said impressively, 'when 'e 'its me, arter I was shoved in, 'e thort I was dahn fer the count. Yus, but orl sailors 'as thick 'eads—in a manner o' speakin'—and when I comes to I hopens one eye quiet-like and sees 'im tinkerin' with a spotlight over a loose board in the corner. In goes 'is 'and, and hout comes the little case o' sparklers, and inter 'is pocket it goes, see?'

'Yes, Ben, I see,' answered Fordyce.

'And then,' proceeded Ben, 'when it's orl dark, and 'e's a-listenin' at the cupboard door, in goes my 'and inter '*is* pocket, hout comes the little case o' sparklers, and inter *my* pocket they goes. Never knew wot they was, o' corse, till I 'as a moment ter look at 'em arterwards—'

'When was that?' asked Fordyce.

'Just afore we comes dahn, guv'nor,' replied Ben. 'While you was hout in the passidge, saying orry-vor to the 'appy family. 'Corse, you'll say now as I was hout ter nab 'em. Blimy if I knows. Things 'appened so quick, I never 'ad time ter think!'

'But you had time to think, Ben,' exclaimed Fordyce warmly, 'when I offered to let you clear out on the stairs.'

'Ah!' nodded Ben. 'I nearly fergot me prayers that time!'

'You could have cleared out then with forty thousand pounds in your pocket!'

'Garn,' retorted Ben uncomfortably. 'Wotcher gettin' at? Tryin' ter make a blinkin' cherubim o' me? I didn't want ter be copped with the stuff, did I? See me goin' inter a bank, chuckin' the sparklers hover the counter, and sayin', "I'll have it in notes!"'

'Nonsense,' laughed Fordyce. 'I agree the necklace might have been an uncomfortable possession, but you're a sport, all the same, and you wanted to get Miss Brant out of a scrape.'

'Ah, yes, wot abart that, now?' exclaimed Ben, turning round. 'Yer ain't goin' back on 'er, are yer, Mr Detective? 'Cos, if yer are, I'll 'ave my sparklers back!'

Fordyce also turned. 'By Jove, Mr Barton—they're wonderful!' he murmured.

'They are, by George,' he replied. 'The Duchess will be a happy woman when she gets them back!'

Fordyce drew a step closer, gazing at the dazzling jewels admiringly.

'Hold them up to the light for a moment, will you?' he asked. 'I've never seen their equal!'

He stared at the diamonds as they were raised—and the next moment, the man who had raised them gave a sharp cry. His wrists were clapped together and something clicked over them.

'What's the meaning of this?' he gasped.

'Keep cool, Detective Barton,' answered Fordyce quietly, as he stooped to regain the necklace, which had slipped to the ground.

'Who the deuce—' spluttered the handcuffed man.

'Or, look here,' continued Fordyce, 'suppose you drop the "Barton" now, and take on your old name of Doyle,' The other stared at him. 'Yes, the game's up, Doyle,' said Fordyce. 'Sorry! You're a shrewd fellow, but you made a couple of bad mistakes. The first was in thinking that the police were only after the necklace—they were also after you.'

'Me? I tell you—'

'Be quiet!' Fordyce's voice was stern. 'Yes, you, Doyle, They were after you, through Sheldrake. They knew that, as sure as the necklace would draw Sheldrake, so Sheldrake would draw you, Mr Henry Doyle.'

The handcuffed man turned, in angry appeal, to the others.

'This is monstrous!' he cried. 'It's all wrong—!'

'Is it? Wait till I've told you of your second mistake, Doyle. Your second mistake was in posing as a detective—and, of all detectives, as Barton. As a matter of fact, I happen to be Barton myself. Rather awkward, isn't it?'

Doyle made no reply. The game was up, and he knew it. Ben, however, took a little longer to convince.

'Wot!' he exclaimed, incredulous and indignant. 'You a real live 'tec—and lettin' me do orl the work?'

'Never mind, Ben!' laughed Fordyce, patting him on the shoulder. 'You'll be mentioned in dispatches! If you want some more work, try and find the way out of this room.' He looked at Miss Brant. 'I'm sorry I had to deceive *you*,' he said.

She had been staring at him as incredulously as Ben. Now she began to understand his attitude, and his veiled allusions. She understood, too, his tenacity. He was no longer a man in the street, who had happened by chance into an empty house, and had fallen there under the spell of adventure and romance . . .

'I—I was a fool!' she murmured, with a catch in her voice. 'I ought to have guessed!'

He went to her quickly. His eyes now looked far more like the eyes of an ordinary man.

'You're guessing wrong,' he answered, 'if you think you're going to suffer by it.'

'What do you mean, Mr Barton?'

'No—it's Fordyce, to you!'

'Mr Fordyce, then.'

'Ah, that's better,' he said, smiling. 'A bit more human, isn't it? Gilbert Fordyce, just an ordinary fellow—who's going to get you out of this. You've got that little bit of paper, haven't you—with my aunt's address?'

'My mind is confused,' she replied. 'This afternoon—everything's got on top of me. I can't understand—'

'Why I'm doing this? Simply can't help myself, that's all. Queer, isn't it? I—I like you! There's very little I don't know about you—I've been watching you from a distance, you see—and I don't believe in clapping people in prison just when they've battled their way out of the mire. No, I simply couldn't do it!'

'But have you thought of your duty?' she asked.

'Duty's a funny thing,' he smiled. 'Yes, I've thought of

it—but sometimes it beats us. If you're thinking of my career, you certainly needn't worry. I've managed a couple of crooks and a diamond necklace in one afternoon—so you won't be missed!'

Ben's voice interrupted their conversation. He had been making fruitless attempts to discover the secret combination which opened the trap-door to the tunnel and the door to the passage, keeping one eye also on Henry Doyle; for, although Doyle was handcuffed, you never really knew where you were with anybody in a house of this sort.

'Guv'nor,' he said hoarsely, ''ave we taken a nine-years' lease o' this plice? Yer know, if I don't git somethink inside me quick, I'll go barmy! I can't hopen the bloomin' thing—' He stopped abruptly, and a frozen grin appeared on his face. 'Oi! Look!' he chattered. 'It's hopenin' of itself!'

'Hallo! Look out!' cried Fordyce.

But Ben did not need the warning. As the floor opened, and the black hole began to yawn, he seized a chair and, raising it above his head, yelled down:

'If yer comes up, I'll 'it yer.'

'Steady with that,' exclaimed Fordyce, and swung him aside as a voice rose from the smoky depths:

'It's only m-m-me!'

Ben dropped the chair, relieved but angry.

'Blimy,' he shouted, 'carn't yer *ever* come in proper through a door?'

A few seconds later Eddie Scott appeared, stuttering and triumphant.

'Inspector and h-half a dozen m-men down there,' he reported. 'They're waiting for you at the Y-y-yard. We've got poor old Brant—he w-walked right into us.'

'Did he?' queried Fordyce, with a glance at Nora.

'Yes. Seems he m-m-missed his train, after all. And, I say—we've g-got Sheldrake, too—with a b-bump on his head the size of an egg.'

'Well done,' replied Fordyce briskly. 'I've not done so badly my end, either. There's Doyle, Eddie. Take him along. And—look!'

He held up the necklace. Eddie's eyes sparkled—not with greed, but with glory. He thumped Fordyce on the back.

'M-m-m-m-magnificent!' he cried.

Then he glanced at Nora, but Fordyce shook his head.

'Nothing more,' said Fordyce quietly. 'Carry on. I'll follow in a minute. Oh, but, first lend me your pocket-book, Eddie, will you?' Eddie handed it over obediently, while Fordyce extracted a bundle of notes. 'Thanks. I'll square the account at the Yard. Now get on with it.'

Eyes were turned upon Henry Doyle. With a shrug, he rose.

''Eave overboard, me 'earty!' chuckled Ben.

Doyle took no notice. He walked quietly to the trap-door, and smiled sourly at Fordyce.

'I nearly had 'em,' he said.

'Yes, you're a sharp fellow—I'll say that for you, Doyle,' answered Fordyce, also smiling, if a trifle grimly. 'In a few years' time, if you're so minded, I may offer you a job.' He watched the rascal go down into the tunnel, and addressed Eddie, who was following. 'Half a minute, Eddie. How's Mr Ackroyd?'

'All fine and b-blooming,' answered Eddie. 'And so's his daughter. I say!'

'Yes?'

'Jolly nice girl, his d-daughter!'

'Rather! She's splendid. You'd better go and tell her so. Hey, wait a second—I've one more question yet. Do you know the combination that opens that door?'

'Of course,' answered Eddie, as he descended. 'Ackroyd told me. N-n-n-number Seventeen.'

Fordyce laughed, while Ben ran to the switch.

'Fancy us not thinking o' that!' Ben guffawed. 'My lucky number! And you a 'tec!' He guffawed again. 'Yer'll be tellin' me as 'ow that stutterin' feller's a 'tec next!'

'So he is,' smiled Fordyce. 'And a damned smart one.'

'Well—I'm blowed,' exclaimed Ben. 'If that ain't the best o' the lot! Swipe me if I don't b'leeve you could turn a 'erring into a 'addock!'

The door swung open. Fordyce walked to Nora, and took her hand.

'That's your way, my child,' he said. 'Not the tunnel for you.'

'Oi, wot abart me?' interposed Ben. 'I ain't a lot gorn on that tunnel meself, guv'nor.'

'You go with her, Ben. Start her on her journey, eh? And'—he handed the sailor a packet of notes—'there's your expenses.'

'Lor' blimey, are we goin' rahnd the bloomin' world?' murmured Ben, staring at the notes. 'I'll look arter 'er, guv'nor—same as I've looked arter you. But we're goin' ter put a square meal in a rahnd 'ole fust!'

He walked to the door, while Nora pressed Fordyce's hand.

'Good-bye,' she said.

'No, only au revoir,' he retorted, as he let her hand go. 'We'll meet again in Normandy.'

She went through the door, and Fordyce, with a smile

of great contentment, began to descend into the tunnel. But a sudden shout made him pause. Ben had come hurrying back.

'Oi!' he called.

'What is it?' asked Fordyce anxiously.

'There's *one* thing yer 'aven't fahnd out yet!' exclaimed Ben.

'Oh! And what's that?'

'Why, 'oo *I* am,' said Ben. 'I'm William the Conk!'

THE END